D0554372

MASHI

AND OTHER STORIES

MASHI

AND OTHER STORIES

BY

Sir RABINDRANATH TAGORE

TRANSLATED FROM THE ORIGINAL BENGALI
BY VARIOUS WRITERS

Short Story Index Reprint Series

BOOKS FOR LIBRARIES PRESS
FREEPORT, NEW YORK

First Published 1918
Reprinted 1972

INTERNATIONAL STANDARD BOOK NUMBER:
0-8369-4123-3

LIBRARY OF CONGRESS CATALOG CARD NUMBER:
70-37564

PRINTED IN THE UNITED STATES OF AMERICA
BY
NEW WORLD BOOK MANUFACTURING CO., INC.
HALLANDALE, FLORIDA 33009

CONTENTS

MASHI

MASHI

I

'Mashi!'[1]

'Try to sleep, Jotin, it is getting late.'

'Never mind if it is. I have not many days left. I was thinking that Mani should go to her father's house.—I forget where he is now.'

'Sitarampur.'

'Oh yes! Sitarampur. Send her there. She should not remain any longer near a sick man. She herself is not strong.'

'Just listen to him! How can she bear to leave you in this state?'

'Does she know what the doctors——?'

'But she can see for herself! The other day she cried her eyes out at the merest hint of having to go to her father's house.'

We must explain that in this statement there

---

[1] The maternal aunt is addressed as Mashi.

3

was a slight distortion of truth, to say the least of it. The actual talk with Mani was as follows :—

'I suppose, my child, you have got some news from your father? I thought I saw your cousin Anath here.'

'Yes! Next Friday will be my little sister's *annaprashan*[1] ceremony. So I'm thinking——'

'All right, my dear. Send her a gold necklace. It will please your mother.'

'I'm thinking of going myself. I've never seen my little sister, and I want to ever so much.'

'Whatever do you mean? You surely don't think of leaving Jotin alone? Haven't you heard what the doctor says about him?'

'But he said that just now there's no special cause for——'

'Even if he did, you can see his state.'

'This is the first girl after three brothers, and she's a great favourite.—I have heard that it's going to be a grand affair. If I don't go, mother will be very——'

'Yes, yes! I don't understand your mother.

---

[1] The *annaprashan* ceremony takes place when a child is first given rice. Usually it receives its name on that day.

But I know very well that your father will be angry enough if you leave Jotin just now.'

'You'll have to write a line to him saying that there is no special cause for anxiety, and that even if I go, there will be no——'

'You're right there ; it will certainly be no great loss if you do go. But remember, if I write to your father, I'll tell him plainly what is in my mind.'

'Then you needn't write. I shall ask my husband, and he will surely——'

'Look here, child, I've borne a good deal from you, but if you do that, I won't stand it for a moment. Your father knows you too well for you to deceive him.'

When Mashi had left her, Mani lay down on her bed in a bad temper.

Her neighbour and friend came and asked what was the matter.

'Look here ! What a shame it is ! Here's my only sister's *annaprashan* coming, and they don't want to let me go to it ! '

'Why ! Surely you're never thinking of going, are you, with your husband so ill ? '

'I don't do anything for him, and I couldn't if

I tried. It's so deadly dull in this house, that I tell you frankly I can't bear it.'

'You are a strange woman!'

'But I can't pretend, as you people do, and look glum lest any one should think ill of me.'

'Well, tell me your plan.'

'I must go. Nobody can prevent me.'

'Isss! What an imperious young woman you are!'

II

Hearing that Mani had wept at the mere thought of going to her father's house, Jotin was so excited that he sat up in bed. Pulling his pillow towards him, he leaned back, and said: 'Mashi, open this window a little, and take that lamp away.'

The still night stood silently at the window like a pilgrim of eternity; and the stars gazed in, witnesses through untold ages of countless death-scenes.

Jotin saw his Mani's face traced on the background of the dark night, and saw those two big dark eyes brimming over with tears, as it were for all eternity.

Mashi felt relieved when she saw him so quiet, thinking he was asleep.

Suddenly he started up, and said : 'Mashi, you all thought that Mani was too frivolous ever to be happy in our house. But you see now——'

'Yes, I see now, my Baba,[1] I was mistaken—but trial tests a person.'

'Mashi!'

'Do try to sleep, dear !'

'Let me think a little, let me talk. Don't be vexed, Mashi !'

'Very well.'

'Once, when I used to think I could not win Mani's heart, I bore it silently. But you——'

'No, dear, I won't allow you to say that; I also bore it.'

'Our minds, you know, are not clods of earth which you can possess by merely picking up. I felt that Mani did not know her own mind, and that one day at some great shock——'

'Yes, Jotin, you are right.'

'Therefore I never took much notice of her waywardness.'

---

[1] Baba literally means Father, but is often used by elders as a term of endearment. In the same way 'Ma' is used.

Mashi remained silent, suppressing a sigh. Not once, but often she had seen Jotin spending the night on the verandah wet with the splashing rain, yet not caring to go into his bedroom. Many a day he lay with a throbbing head, longing, she knew, that Mani would come and soothe his brow, while Mani was getting ready to go to the theatre. Yet when Mashi went to fan him, he sent her away petulantly. She alone knew what pain lay hidden in that distress. Again and again she had wanted to say to Jotin : 'Don't pay so much attention to that silly child, my dear ; let her learn to want, —to cry for things.' But these things cannot be said, and are apt to be misunderstood. Jotin had in his heart a shrine set up to the goddess Woman, and there Mani had her throne. It was hard for him to imagine that his own fate was to be denied his share of the wine of love poured out by that divinity. Therefore the worship went on, the sacrifice was offered, and the hope of a boon never ceased.

Mashi imagined once more that Jotin was sleeping, when he cried out suddenly :

'I know you thought that I was not happy with Mani, and therefore you were angry with her.

But, Mashi, happiness is like those stars. They don't cover all the darkness; there are gaps between. We make mistakes in life and we misunderstand, and yet there remain gaps through which truth shines. I do not know whence comes this gladness that fills my heart to-night.'

Mashi began gently to soothe Jotin's brow, her tears unseen in the dark.

' I was thinking, Mashi, she's so young ! What will she do when I am——? '

' Young, Jotin? She's old enough. I too was young when I lost the idol of my life, only to find him in my heart for ever. Was that any loss, do you think? Besides, is happiness absolutely necessary? '

' Mashi, it seems as if just when Mani's heart shows signs of awakening I have to—— '

' Don't you worry about that, Jotin. Isn't it enough if her heart awakes? '

Suddenly Jotin recollected the words of a village minstrel's song which he had heard long before :

O my heart! you woke not when the man of my heart came to my door.

At the sound of his departing steps you woke up.

Oh, you woke up in the dark !

'Mashi, what is the time now?'

'About nine.'

'So early as that! Why, I thought it must be at least two or three o'clock. My midnight, you know, begins at sundown. But why did you want me to sleep, then?'

'Why, you know how late last night you kept awake talking; so to-day you must get to sleep early.'

'Is Mani asleep?'

'Oh no, she's busy making some soup for you.'

'You don't mean to say so, Mashi? Does she—— ?'

'Certainly! Why, she prepares all your food, the busy little woman.'

'I thought perhaps Mani could not——'

'It doesn't take long for a woman to learn such things. With the need it comes of itself.'

'The fish soup, that I had in the morning, had such a delicate flavour, I thought you had made it.'

'Dear me, no! Surely you don't think Mani would let me do anything for you? Why, she does all your washing herself. She knows you can't bear anything dirty about you. If only you could see your sitting-room, how spick and span she keeps it! If I were to let her haunt your sick-room, she would wear herself out. But that's what she really wants to do.'

' Is Mani's health, then——— ? '

' The doctors think she should not be allowed to visit the sick-room too often. She's too tender-hearted.'

'But, Mashi, how do you prevent her from coming ? '

'Because she obeys me implicitly. But still I have constantly to be giving her news of you.'

The stars glistened in the sky like tear-drops. Jotin bowed his head in gratitude to his life that was about to depart, and when Death stretched out his right hand towards him through the darkness, he took it in perfect trust.

Jotin sighed, and, with a slight gesture of impatience, said :

' Mashi, if Mani is still awake, then, could I —if only for a——— ? '

' Very well ! I'll go and call her.'

' I won't keep her long, only for five minutes. I have something particular to tell her.'

Mashi, sighing, went out to call Mani. Meanwhile Jotin's pulse began to beat fast. He knew too well that he had never been able to have an intimate talk with Mani. The two instruments were tuned differently and it was not easy to play them in unison. Again and again, Jotin had felt pangs of jealousy on hearing Mani chattering and laughing merrily with her girl companions. Jotin blamed only himself,—why couldn't he talk irrelevant trifles as they did? Not that he could not, for with his men friends he often chatted on all sorts of trivialities. But the small talk that suits men is not suitable for women. You can hold a philosophical discourse in monologue, ignoring your inattentive audience altogether, but small talk requires the co-operation of at least two. The bagpipes can be played singly, but there must be a pair of cymbals. How often in the evenings had Jotin, when sitting on the open verandah with Mani, made some strained attempts at conversation, only to feel the thread snap. And the very silence of the evening felt ashamed. Jotin was certain that Mani longed to get away. He had even wished earnestly that a third person would come. For talking is easy with three, when it is hard for two.

He began to think what he should say when
Mani came. But such manufactured talk would
not satisfy him. Jotin felt afraid that this five
minutes of to-night would be wasted. Yet, for
him, there were but few moments left for intimate
talk.

III

'What's this, child, you're not going anywhere,
are you?'

'Of course, I'm going to Sitarampur.'

'What do you mean? Who is going to take
you?'

'Anath.'

'Not to-day, my child, some other day.'

'But the compartment has already been re-
served.'

'What does that matter? That loss can easily
be borne. Go to-morrow, early in the morning.'

'Mashi, I don't hold by your inauspicious
days. What harm if I do go to-day?'

'Jotin wants to have a talk with you.'

'All right! there's still some time. I'll just
go and see him.'

'But you mustn't say that you are going.'

'Very well, I won't tell him, but I shan't be

able to stay long.   To-morrow is my sister's
annaprashan, and I must go to-day.'

'Oh, my child! I beg you to listen to
me this once.   Quiet your mind for a while
and sit by him.   Don't let him see your
hurry.'

'What can I do? The train won't wait for
me.   Anath will be back in ten minutes.   I can
sit by him till then.'

'No, that won't do.   I shall never let you go
to him in that frame of mind. . . . Oh, you
wretch! the man you are torturing is soon to leave
this world ; but I warn you, you will remember
this day till the end of your days!   That there is
a God! that there is a God! you will some day
understand!'

'Mashi, you mustn't curse me like that.'

'Oh, my darling boy! my darling! why do
you go on living longer?   There is no end to
this sin, yet I cannot check it!'

Mashi after delaying a little returned to the
sick-room, hoping by that time Jotin would be
asleep.   But Jotin moved in his bed when she
entered.   Mashi exclaimed :

'Just look what she has done!'

'What's happened? Hasn't Mani come? Why have you been so long, Mashi?'

'I found her weeping bitterly because she had allowed the milk for your soup to get burnt! I tried to console her, saying, "Why, there's more milk to be had!" But that she could be so careless about the preparation of *your* soup made her wild. With great trouble I managed to pacify her and put her to bed. So I haven't brought her to-day. Let her sleep it off.'

Though Jotin was pained when Mani didn't come, yet he felt a certain amount of relief. He had half feared that Mani's bodily presence would do violence to his heart's image of her. Such things had happened before in his life. And the gladness of the idea that Mani was miserable at burning *his* milk filled his heart to overflowing.

'Mashi!'

'What is it, Baba?'

'I feel quite certain that my days are drawing to a close. But I have no regrets. Don't grieve for me.'

'No, dear, I won't grieve. I don't believe that only life is good and not death.'

'Mashi, I tell you truly that death seems sweet.'

Jotin, gazing at the dark sky, felt that it was Mani herself who was coming to him in Death's guise. She had immortal youth and the stars were flowers of blessing, showered upon her dark tresses by the hand of the World-Mother. It seemed as if once more he had his first sight of his bride under the veil of darkness.[1] The immense night became filled with the loving gaze of Mani's dark eyes. Mani, the bride of this house, the little girl, became transformed into a world-image,—her throne on the altar of the stars at the confluence of life and death. Jotin said to himself with clasped hands : 'At last the veil is raised, the covering is rent in this deep darkness. Ah, beautiful one! how often have you wrung my heart, but no longer shall you forsake me!'

IV

'I'm suffering, Mashi, but nothing like you imagine. It seems to me as if my pain were gradually separating itself from my life. Like a laden boat, it was so long being towed behind, but the rope has snapped, and now it floats away with all my burdens. Still I can see it, but it is no

[1] The bride and the bridegroom see each other's face for the first time at the marriage ceremony under a veil thrown over their heads.

longer mine. . . . But, Mashi, I've not seen Mani even once for the last two days!'

'Jotin, let me give you another pillow.'

'It almost seems to me, Mashi, that Mani also has left me like that laden boat of sorrow which drifts away.'

'Just sip some pomegranate juice, dear! Your throat must be getting dry.'

'I wrote my will yesterday; did I show it to you? I can't recollect.'

'There's no need to show it to me, Jotin.'

'When mother died, I had nothing of my own. You fed me and brought me up. Therefore I was saying——'

'Nonsense, child! I had only this house and a little property. You earned the rest.'

'But this house—— ?'

'That's nothing. Why, you've added to it so much that it's difficult to find out where my house was!'

'I'm sure Mani's love for you is really——'

'Yes, yes! I know that, Jotin. Now you try to sleep.'

'Though I have bequeathed all my property to Mani, it is practically yours, Mashi. She will never disobey you.'

C

'Why are you worrying so much about that, dear?'

'All I have I owe to you. When you see my will don't think for a moment that——'

'What do you mean, Jotin? Do you think I shall mind for a moment because you give to Mani what belongs to you? Surely I'm not so mean as that?'

'But you also will have——'

'Look here, Jotin, I shall get angry with you. You want to console me with money!'

'Oh, Mashi, how I wish I could give you something better than money!'

'That you have done, Jotin!—more than enough. Haven't I had you to fill my lonely house? I must have won that great good-fortune in many previous births! You have given me so much that now, if my destiny's due is exhausted, I shall not complain. Yes, yes! Give away everything in Mani's name,—your house, your money, your carriage, and your land—such burdens are too heavy for me!'

'Of course I know you have lost your taste for the enjoyments of life, but Mani is so young that——'

'No! you mustn't say that. If you want to

leave her your property, it is all right, but as for enjoyment—— '

' What harm if she does enjoy herself, Mashi ? '

' No, no, it will be impossible. Her throat will become parched, and it will be dust and ashes to her.'

Jotin remained silent. He could not decide whether it was true or not, and whether it was a matter of regret or otherwise, that the world would become distasteful to Mani for want of him. The stars seemed to whisper in his heart :

' Indeed it is true. We have been watching for thousands of years, and know that all these great preparations for enjoyment are but vanity.'

Jotin sighed and said : ' We cannot leave behind us what is really worth giving.'

' It's no trifle you are giving, dearest. I only pray she may have the power to know the value of what is given her.'

' Give me a little more of that pomegranate juice, Mashi, I'm thirsty. Did Mani come to me yesterday, I wonder ? '

' Yes, she came, but you were asleep. She sat

by your head, fanning you for a long time, and then went away to get your clothes washed.'

'How wonderful! I believe I was dreaming that very moment that Mani was trying to enter my room. The door was slightly open, and she was pushing against it, but it wouldn't open. But, Mashi, you're going too far,—you ought to let her see that I am dying ; otherwise my death will be a terrible shock to her.'

'Baba, let me put this shawl over your feet ; they are getting cold.'

'No, Mashi, I can't bear anything over me like that.'

'Do you know, Jotin, Mani made this shawl for you ? When she ought to have been asleep, she was busy at it. It was finished only yesterday.'

Jotin took the shawl, and touched it tenderly with his hands. It seemed to him that the softness of the wool was Mani's own. Her loving thoughts had been woven night after night with its threads. It was not made merely of wool, but also of her touch. Therefore, when Mashi drew that shawl over his feet, it seemed as if, night after night, Mani had been caressing his tired limbs.

'But, Mashi, I thought Mani didn't know how to knit,—at any rate she never liked it.'

'It doesn't take long to learn a thing. Of course I had to teach her. Then there are a good many mistakes in it.'

'Let there be mistakes; we're not going to send it to the Paris Exhibition. It will keep my feet warm in spite of its mistakes.'

Jotin's mind began to picture Mani at her task, blundering and struggling, and yet patiently going on night after night. How sweetly pathetic it was! And again he went over the shawl with his caressing fingers.

'Mashi, is the doctor downstairs?'

'Yes, he will stay here to-night.'

'But tell him it is useless for him to give me a sleeping draught. It doesn't bring me real rest and only adds to my pain. Let me remain properly awake. Do you know, Mashi, that my wedding took place on the night of the full moon in the month of *Baisakh*? To-morrow will be that day, and the stars of that very night will be shining in the sky. Mani perhaps has forgotten. I want to remind her of it to-day; just call her to me for a minute or two. . . . Why do you keep silent? I suppose the doctor has told you I am so weak that any excitement will—— but I tell you truly, Mashi, to-night, if I can have only a few minutes'

talk with her, there will be no need for any
sleeping draughts. Mashi, don't cry like that!
I am quite well. To-day my heart is full as it has
never been in my life before. That's why I want
to see Mani. No, no, Mashi, I can't bear to
see you crying! You have been so quiet all these
last days. Why are you so troubled to-night?'

'Oh, Jotin, I thought that I had exhausted all
my tears, but I find there are plenty left. I can't
bear it any longer.'

'Call Mani. I'll remind her of our wedding
night, so that to-morrow she may——'

'I'm going, dear. Shombhu will wait at the
door. If you want anything, call him.'

Mashi went to Mani's bedroom and sat down
on the floor crying,—'Oh come, come once, you
heartless wretch! Keep his last request who has
given you his all! Don't kill him who is already
dying!'

Jotin hearing the sound of footsteps started up,
saying, 'Mani!'

'I am Shombhu. Did you call me?'

'Ask your mistress to come?'

'Ask whom?'

'Your mistress.'

'She has not yet returned.'

'Returned? From where?'

'From Sitarampur.'

'When did she go?'

'Three days ago.'

For a moment Jotin felt numb all over, and his head began to swim. He slipped down from the pillows, on which he was reclining, and kicked off the woollen shawl that was over his feet.

When Mashi came back after a long time, Jotin did not mention Mani's name, and Mashi thought he had forgotten all about her.

Suddenly Jotin cried out: 'Mashi, did I tell you about the dream I had the other night?'

'Which dream?'

'That in which Mani was pushing the door, and the door wouldn't open more than an inch. She stood outside unable to enter. Now I know that Mani has to stand outside my door till the last.'

Mashi kept silent. She realised that the heaven she had been building for Jotin out of falsehood had toppled down at last. If sorrow comes, it is best to acknowledge it.—When God strikes, we cannot avoid the blow.

'Mashi, the love I have got from you will last through all my births. I have filled this life with it to carry it with me. In the next birth, I am sure you will be born as my daughter, and I shall tend you with all my love.'

'What are you saying, Jotin? Do you mean to say I shall be born again as a woman? Why can't you pray that I should come to your arms as a son?'

'No, no, not a son! You will come to my house in that wonderful beauty which you had when you were young. I can even imagine how I shall dress you.'

'Don't talk so much, Jotin, but try to sleep.'

'I shall name you "Lakshmi."'

'But that is an old-fashioned name, Jotin!'

'Yes, but you are my old-fashioned Mashi. Come to my house again with those beautiful old-fashioned manners.'

'I can't wish that I should come and burden your home with the misfortune of a girl-child!'

'Mashi, you think me weak, and are wanting to save me all trouble.'

'My child, I am a woman, so I have my weakness. Therefore I have tried all my life to save you from all sorts of trouble,—only to fail.'

'Mashi, I have not had time in this life to apply the lessons I have learnt. But they will keep for my next birth. I shall show then what a man is able to do. I have learnt how false it is always to be looking after oneself.'

'Whatever you may say, darling, you have never grasped anything for yourself, but given everything to others.'

'Mashi, I can boast of one thing at any rate. I have never been a tyrant in my happiness, or tried to enforce my claims by violence. Because lies could not content me, I have had to wait long. Perhaps truth will be kind to me at last.—Who is that, Mashi, who is that?'

'Where? There's no one there, Jotin!'

'Mashi, just go and see in the other room. I thought I——'

'No, dear! I don't see anybody.'

'But it seemed quite clear to me that——'

'No, Jotin, it's nothing. So keep quiet! The doctor is coming now.'

When the doctor entered, he said:

'Look here, you mustn't stay near the patient so much, you excite him. You go to bed, and my assistant will remain with him.'

'No, Mashi, I can't let you go.'

'All right, Baba! I will sit quietly in that corner.'

'No, no! you must sit by my side. I can't let go your hand, not till the very end. I have been made by your hand, and only from your hand shall God take me.'

'All right,' said the doctor, 'you can remain there. But, Jotin Babu, you must not talk to her. It's time for you to take your medicine.'

'Time for my medicine? Nonsense! The time for that is over. To give medicine now is merely to deceive; besides I am not afraid to die. Mashi, Death is busy with his physic; why do you add another nuisance in the shape of a doctor? Send him away, send him away! It is you alone I need now! No one else, none whatever! No more falsehood!'

'I protest, as a doctor, this excitement is doing you harm.'

'Then go, doctor, don't excite me any more! —Mashi, has he gone? . . . That's good! Now come and take my head in your lap.'

'All right, dear! Now, Baba, try to sleep!'

'No, Mashi, don't ask me to sleep. If I sleep, I shall never wake. I still need to keep awake a little longer. Don't you hear a sound? Somebody is coming.'

V

' Jotin dear, just open your eyes a little. She has come.   Look once and see ! '

' Who has come ?   A dream ? '

' Not a dream, darling !   Mani has come with her father.'

' Who are you ? '

' Can't you see ?   This is your Mani ! '

' Mani ?   Has that door opened ? '

' Yes, Baba, it is wide open.'

' No, Mashi, not that shawl ! not *that* shawl! That shawl is a fraud ! '

' It is not a shawl, Jotin !   It is our Mani, who has flung herself on your feet. Put your hand on her head and bless her.   Don't cry like that, Mani !   There will be time enough for that. Keep quiet now for a little.'

THE SKELETON

THE SKELETON

In the room next to the one in which we boys used to sleep, there hung a human skeleton. In the night it would rattle in the breeze which played about its bones. In the day these bones were rattled by us. We were taking lessons in osteology from a student in the Campbell Medical School, for our guardians were determined to make us masters of all the sciences. How far they succeeded we need not tell those who know us ; and it is better hidden from those who do not.

Many years have passed since then. In the meantime the skeleton has vanished from the room, and the science of osteology from our brains, leaving no trace behind.

The other day, our house was crowded with guests, and I had to pass the night in the same old room. In these now unfamiliar surroundings, sleep refused to come, and, as I tossed from side to side, I heard all the hours of the night chimed, one

after another, by the church clock near by.　At
length the lamp in the corner of the room, after
some minutes of choking and spluttering, went
out altogether.　One or two bereavements had
recently happened in the family, so the going
out of the lamp naturally led me to thoughts of
death.　In the great arena of nature, I thought,
the light of a lamp losing itself in eternal darkness, and the going out of the light of our little
human lives, by day or by night, were much the
same thing.

My train of thought recalled to my mind the
skeleton.　While I was trying to imagine what
the body which had clothed it could have been
like, it suddenly seemed to me that something was
walking round and round my bed, groping along
the walls of the room.　I could hear its rapid
breathing.　It seemed as if it was searching for
something which it could not find, and pacing
round the room with ever-hastier steps.　I felt
quite sure that this was a mere fancy of my sleepless, excited brain ; and that the throbbing of the
veins in my temples was really the sound which
seemed like running footsteps.　Nevertheless, a
cold shiver ran all over me.　To help to get rid
of this hallucination, I called out aloud : ' Who is

there ? ' The footsteps seemed to stop at my bed-side, and the reply came : ' It is I. I have come to look for that skeleton of mine.'

It seemed absurd to show any fear before the creature of my own imagination ; so, clutching my pillow a little more tightly, I said in a casual sort of way : ' A nice business for this time of night ! Of what use will that skeleton be to you now ? '

The reply seemed to come almost from my mosquito-curtain itself. ' What a question ! In that skeleton were the bones that encircled my heart ; the youthful charm of my six-and-twenty years bloomed about it. Should I not desire to see it once more? '

' Of course,' said I, ' a perfectly reasonable desire. Well, go on with your search, while I try to get a little sleep.'

Said the voice : ' But I fancy you are lonely. All right ; I'll sit down a while, and we will have a little chat. Years ago I used to sit by men and talk to them. But during the last thirty-five years I have only moaned in the wind in the burning-places of the dead. I would talk once more with a man as in the old times.'

I felt that some one sat down just near my

D

curtain. Resigning myself to the situation, I replied with as much cordiality as I could summon :
'That will be very nice indeed. Let us talk of something cheerful.'

'The funniest thing I can think of is my own life-story. Let me tell you that.'

The church clock chimed the hour of two.

'When I was in the land of the living, and young, I feared one thing like death itself, and that was my husband. My feelings can be likened only to those of a fish caught with a hook. For it was as if a stranger had snatched me away with the sharpest of hooks from the peaceful calm of my childhood's home—and from him I had no means of escape. My husband died two months after my marriage, and my friends and relations moaned pathetically on my behalf. My husband's father, after scrutinising my face with great care, said to my mother-in-law : "Do you not see, she has the evil eye?"—Well, are you listening ? I hope you are enjoying the story ? '

'Very much indeed ! ' said I. 'The beginning is extremely humorous.'

'Let me proceed then. I came back to my father's house in great glee. People tried to conceal it from me, but I knew well that I was

endowed with a rare and radiant beauty. What
is your opinion ? '

'Very likely,' I murmured. 'But you must
remember that I never saw you.'

'What ! Not seen me ? What about that
skeleton of mine ? Ha ! ha ! ha ! Never mind.
I was only joking. How can I ever make you
believe that those two cavernous hollows contained
the brightest of dark, languishing eyes ? And
that the smile which was revealed by those ruby
lips had no resemblance whatever to the grinning
teeth which you used to see ? The mere attempt
to convey to you some idea of the grace, the
charm, the soft, firm, dimpled curves, which in the
fulness of youth were growing and blossoming
over those dry old bones makes me smile ; it also
makes me angry. The most eminent doctors of
my time could not have dreamed of the bones
of that body of mine as materials for teaching
osteology. Do you know, one young doctor that
I knew of, actually compared me to a golden
champak blossom. It meant that to him the
rest of humankind was fit only to illustrate the
science of physiology, that I was a flower of beauty.
Does any one think of the skeleton of a *champak*
flower ?

'When I walked, I felt that, like a diamond scattering splendour, my every movement set waves of beauty radiating on every side. I used to spend hours gazing on my hands—hands which could gracefully have reined the liveliest of male creatures.

'But that stark and staring old skeleton of mine has borne false-witness to you against me, while I was unable to refute the shameless libel. That is why of all men I hate you most! I feel I would like once for all to banish sleep from your eyes with a vision of that warm rosy loveliness of mine, to sweep out with it all the wretched osteological stuff of which your brain is full.'

'I could have sworn by your body,' cried I, 'if you had it still, that no vestige of osteology has remained in my head, and that the only thing that it is now full of is a radiant vision of perfect loveliness, glowing against the black background of night. I cannot say more than that.'

'I had no girl-companions,' went on the voice. 'My only brother had made up his mind not to marry. In the zenana I was alone. Alone I used to sit in the garden under the shade of the trees, and dream that the whole world was in love with me ; that the stars with sleepless gaze were drinking in my beauty ; that the wind was languishing in sighs as on some pretext or other it brushed past me ; and that the lawn on which my feet rested, had it been conscious, would have lost consciousness again at their touch. It seemed to me that all the young men in the world were as blades of grass at my feet ; and my heart, I know not why, used to grow sad.

' When my brother's friend, Shekhar, had passed out of the Medical College, he became our family doctor. I had already often seen him from behind a curtain. My brother was a strange man, and did not care to look on the world with open eyes. It was not empty enough for his taste ; so he gradually moved away from it, until he was quite lost in an obscure corner. Shekhar was his one friend, so he was the only young man I could ever get to see. And when I held my evening court in my garden, then the host of imaginary young men whom I had at my feet were each one a Shekhar.—Are you listening ? What are you thinking of ? '

I sighed as I replied : ' I was wishing I was Shekhar ! '

' Wait a bit. Hear the whole story first. One day, in the rains, I was feverish. The doctor

came to see me.   That was our first meeting.   I
was reclining opposite the window, so that the
blush of the evening sky might temper the pallor
of my complexion.   When the doctor, coming in,
looked up into my face, I put myself into his place,
and gazed at myself in imagination.   I saw in the
glorious evening light that delicate wan face laid
like a drooping flower against the soft white pillow,
with the unrestrained curls playing over the forehead, and the bashfully lowered eyelids casting a
pathetic shade over the whole countenance.

'The doctor, in a tone bashfully low, asked
my brother : " Might I feel her pulse ? "

'I put out a tired, well-rounded wrist from
beneath the coverlet. "Ah!" thought I, as I looked
on it, " if only there had been a sapphire bracelet." [1]
I have never before seen a doctor so awkward
about feeling a patient's pulse.   His fingers
trembled as they felt my wrist.   He measured the
heat of my fever, I gauged the pulse of his heart.
—Don't you believe me ? '

'Very easily,' said I ; 'the human heart-beat
tells its tale.'

'After I had been taken ill and restored to

[1] Widows are supposed to dress in white only, without ornaments or
jewellery.

health several times, I found that the number of
the courtiers who attended my imaginary evening
reception began to dwindle till they were reduced
to only one ! And at last in my little world there
remained only one doctor and one patient.

'In these evenings I used to dress myself[1]
secretly in a canary-coloured *sari* ; twine about the
braided knot into which I did my hair a garland
of white jasmine blossoms ; and with a little
mirror in my hand betake myself to my usual seat
under the trees.

'Well ! Are you perhaps thinking that the
sight of one's own beauty would soon grow
wearisome? Ah no ! for I did not see myself
with my own eyes. I was then one and also two.
I used to see myself as though I were the doctor ;
I gazed, I was charmed, I fell madly in love.
But, in spite of all the caresses I lavished on myself, a sigh would wander about my heart, moaning
like the evening breeze.

'Anyhow, from that time I was never alone.
When I walked I watched with downcast eyes the
play of my dainty little toes on the earth, and
wondered what the doctor would have felt had he
been there to see. At mid-day the sky would be

[1] See note on p. 38.

filled with the glare of the sun, without a sound, save now and then the distant cry of a passing kite. Outside our garden-walls the hawker would pass with his musical cry of "Bangles for sale, crystal bangles." And I, spreading a snow-white sheet on the lawn, would lie on it with my head on my arm. With studied carelessness the other arm would rest lightly on the soft sheet, and I would imagine to myself that some one had caught sight of the wonderful pose of my hand, that some one had clasped it in both of his and imprinted a kiss on its rosy palm, and was slowly walking away.—What if I ended the story here? How would it do?'

'Not half a bad ending,' I replied thoughtfully. 'It would no doubt remain a little incomplete, but I could easily spend the rest of the night putting in the finishing touches.'

'But that would make the story too serious. Where would the laugh come in? Where would be the skeleton with its grinning teeth?

'So let me go on. As soon as the doctor had got a little practice, he took a room on the ground-floor of our house for a consulting-chamber. I used then sometimes to ask him jokingly about medicines and poisons, and how much of this drug or that would kill a man. The subject was congenial and he would wax eloquent. These talks familiarised me with the idea of death ; and so love and death were the only two things that filled my little world. My story is now nearly ended—there is not much left.'

'Not much of the night is left either,' I muttered.

'After a time I noticed that the doctor had grown strangely absent-minded, and it seemed as if he were ashamed of something which he was trying to keep from me. One day he came in, somewhat smartly dressed, and borrowed my brother's carriage for the evening.

'My curiosity became too much for me, and I went up to my brother for information. After some talk beside the point, I at last asked him : "By the way, Dada,[1] where is the doctor going this evening in your carriage ?"

'My brother briefly replied : "To his death."

'"Oh, do tell me," I importuned. "Where is he really going?"

'"To be married," he said, a little more explicitly.

'"Oh, indeed !" said I, as I laughed long and loudly.

---

[1] Elder brother.

'I gradually learnt that the bride was an heiress, who would bring the doctor a large sum of money. But why did he insult me by hiding all this from me ? Had I ever begged and prayed him not to marry, because it would break my heart? Men are not to be trusted. I have known only one man in all my life, and in a moment I made this discovery.

'When the doctor came in after his work and was ready to start, I said to him, rippling with laughter the while : " Well, doctor, so you are to be married to-night ? "

'My gaiety not only made the doctor lose countenance ; it thoroughly irritated him.

'"How is it," I went on, "that there is no illumination, no band of music ? "

'With a sigh he replied : " Is marriage then such a joyful occasion ? "

'I burst out into renewed laughter. "No, no," said I, "this will never do. Who ever heard of a wedding without lights and music ? "

I bothered my brother about it so much that he at once ordered all the trappings of a gay wedding.

'All the time I kept on gaily talking of the bride, of what would happen, of what I would do when the bride came home. "And, doctor," I asked, "will you still go on feeling pulses?" Ha! ha! ha! Though the inner workings of people's, especially men's, minds are not visible, still I can take my oath that these words were piercing the doctor's bosom like deadly darts.

'The marriage was to be celebrated late at night. Before starting, the doctor and my brother were having a glass of wine together on the terrace, as was their daily habit. The moon had just risen.

'I went up smiling, and said: "Have you forgotten your wedding, doctor? It is time to start."

'I must here tell you one little thing. I had meanwhile gone down to the dispensary and got a little powder, which at a convenient opportunity I had dropped unobserved into the doctor's glass.

'The doctor, draining his glass at a gulp, in a voice thick with emotion, and with a look that pierced me to the heart, said: "Then I must go."

'The music struck up. I went into my room and dressed myself in my bridal-robes of silk and gold. I took out my jewellery and ornaments from the safe and put them all on; I put the red mark of wifehood on the parting in my hair. And then under the tree in the garden I prepared my bed.

'It was a beautiful night. The gentle south wind was kissing away the weariness of the world. The scent of jasmine and *bela* filled the garden with rejoicing.

'When the sound of the music began to grow fainter and fainter ; the light of the moon to get dimmer and dimmer ; the world with its lifelong associations of home and kin to fade away from my perceptions like some illusion ;—then I closed my eyes, and smiled.

'I fancied that when people came and found me they would see that smile of mine lingering on my lips like a trace of rose-coloured wine, that when I thus slowly entered my eternal bridal-chamber I should carry with me this smile, illuminating my face. But alas for the bridal-chamber ! Alas for the bridal-robes of silk and gold ! When I woke at the sound of a rattling within me, I found three urchins learning osteology from my skeleton. Where in my bosom my joys and griefs used to throb, and the petals of youth to open one by one, there the master with his pointer was busy naming my bones. And as to that last smile, which I had so carefully rehearsed, did you see any sign of that ?

'Well, well, how did you like the story ? '

'It has been delightful,' said I.

At this point the first crow began to caw.
'Are you there?' I asked.   There was no reply.

The morning light entered the room.

THE AUSPICIOUS VISION

THE AUSPICIOUS VISION

KANTICHANDRA was young; yet after his wife's death he sought no second partner, and gave his mind to the hunting of beasts and birds. His body was long and slender, hard and agile; his sight keen; his aim unerring. He dressed like a countryman, and took with him Hira Singh the wrestler, Chakkanlal, Khan Saheb the musician, Mian Saheb, and many others. He had no lack of idle followers.

In the month of *Agrahayan* Kanti had gone out shooting near the swamp of Nydighi with a few sporting companions. They were in boats, and an army of servants, in boats also, filled the bathing-*ghats*. The village women found it well-nigh impossible to bathe or to draw water. All day long, land and water trembled to the firing of the guns; and every evening musicians killed the chance of sleep.

One morning as Kanti was seated in his boat

cleaning a favourite gun, he suddenly started at what he thought was the cry of wild duck.   Looking up, he saw a village maiden, coming to the water's edge, with two white ducklings clasped to her breast.   The little stream was almost stagnant. Many weeds choked the current.   The girl put the birds into the water, and watched them anxiously.   Evidently the presence of the sportsmen was the cause of her care and not the wildness of the ducks.

The girl's beauty had a rare freshness—as if she had just come from Vishwakarma's [1] workshop. It was difficult to guess her age.   Her figure was almost a woman's, but her face was so childish that clearly the world had left no impression there. She seemed not to know herself that she had reached the threshold of youth.

Kanti's gun-cleaning stopped for a while.   He was fascinated.   He had not expected to see such a face in such a spot.   And yet its beauty suited its surroundings better than it would have suited a palace.   A bud is lovelier on the bough than in a golden vase.   That day the blossoming reeds glittered in the autumn dew and morning sun, and the fresh, simple face set in the midst was like a

---

[1] The divine craftsman in Hindu mythology.

picture of festival to Kanti's enchanted mind. Kalidos has forgotten to sing how Siva's Mountain-Queen herself sometimes has come to the young Ganges, with just such ducklings in her breast. As he gazed, the maiden started in terror, and hurriedly took back the ducks into her bosom with a half-articulate cry of pain. In another moment, she had left the river-bank and disappeared into the bamboo thicket hard by. Looking round, Kanti saw one of his men pointing an unloaded gun at the ducks. He at once went up to him, wrenched away his gun, and bestowed on his cheek a prodigious slap. The astonished humourist finished his joke on the floor. Kanti went on cleaning his gun.

But curiosity drove Kanti to the thicket wherein he had seen the girl disappear. Pushing his way through, he found himself in the yard of a well-to-do householder. On one side was a row of conical thatched barns, on the other a clean cow-shed, at the end of which grew a *zizyph* bush. Under the bush was seated the girl he had seen that morning, sobbing over a wounded dove, into whose yellow beak she was trying to wring a little water from the moist corner of her garment. A grey cat, its fore-paws on her knee, was looking eagerly at the bird, and every now and then, when it got too forward, she kept it in its place by a warning tap on the nose.

This little picture, set in the peaceful mid-day surroundings of the householder's yard, instantly impressed itself on Kanti's sensitive heart. The checkered light and shade, flickering beneath the delicate foliage of the *zizyph*, played on the girl's lap. Not far off a cow was chewing the cud, and lazily keeping off the flies with slow movements of its head and tail. The north wind whispered softly in the rustling bamboo thickets. And she who at dawn on the river-bank had looked like the Forest Queen, now in the silence of noon showed the eager pity of the Divine Housewife. Kanti, coming in upon her with his gun, had a sense of intrusion. He felt like a thief caught red-handed. He longed to explain that it was not he who had hurt the dove. As he wondered how he should begin, there came a call of ' Sudha ! ' from the house. The girl jumped up. ' Sudha! ' came the voice again. She took up her dove, and ran within. ' Sudha,'[1] thought Kanti, ' what an appropriate name ! '

Kanti returned to the boat, handed his gun to

[1] *Sudha* means nectar, ambrosia.

his men, and went over to the front door of the house. He found a middle-aged Brahmin, with a peaceful, clean-shaven face, seated on a bench outside, and reading a devotional book. Kanti saw in his kindly, thoughtful face something of the tenderness which shone in the face of the maiden.

Kanti saluted him, and said : ' May I ask for some water, sir ? I am very thirsty.' The elder man welcomed him with eager hospitality, and, offering him a seat on the bench, went inside and fetched with his own hands a little brass plate of sugar wafers and a bell-metal vessel full of water.

After Kanti had eaten and drunk, the Brahmin begged him to introduce himself. Kanti gave his own name, his father's name, and the address of his home, and then said in the usual way : ' If I can be of any service, sir, I shall deem myself fortunate.'

' I require no service, my son,' said Nabin Banerji ; ' I have only one care at present.'

' What is that, sir ? ' said Kanti.

' It is my daughter, Sudha, who is growing up ' (Kanti smiled as he thought of her babyish face), ' and for whom I have not yet been able to find a worthy bridegroom. If I could only see her well married, all my debt to this world would be paid. But there is no suitable bridegroom here, and I cannot leave my charge of Gopinath here, to search for a husband elsewhere.'

'If you would see me in my boat, sir, we would have a talk about the marriage of your daughter.' So saying, Kanti repeated his salute and went back. He then sent some of his men into the village to inquire, and in answer heard nothing but praise of the beauty and virtues of the Brahmin's daughter.

When next day the old man came to the boat on his promised visit, Kanti bent low in salutation, and begged the hand of his daughter for himself. The Brahmin was so much overcome by this undreamed-of piece of good fortune—for Kanti not only belonged to a well-known Brahmin family, but was also a landed proprietor of wealth and position—that at first he could hardly utter a word in reply. He thought there must have been some mistake, and at length mechanically repeated: 'You desire to marry my daughter ?'

'If you will deign to give her to me,' said Kanti.

'You mean Sudha ?' he asked again.

'Yes,' was the reply.

'But will you not first see and speak to her——?'

Kanti, pretending he had not seen her already, said : 'Oh, that we shall do at the moment of the Auspicious Vision.'[1]

In a voice husky with emotion the old man said : 'My Sudha is indeed a good girl, well skilled in all the household arts.   As you are so generously taking her on trust, may she never cause you a moment's regret.   This is my blessing !'

The brick-built mansion of the Mazumdars had been borrowed for the wedding ceremony, which was fixed for next *Magh*, as Kanti did not wish to delay.   In due time the bridegroom arrived on his elephant, with drums and music and with a torchlight procession, and the ceremony began.

When the bridal couple were covered with the scarlet screen for the rite of the Auspicious Vision, Kanti looked up at his bride.   In that bashful, downcast face, crowned with the wedding coronet and bedecked with sandal paste, he could scarcely recognise the village maiden of his fancy, and in

---

[1] After betrothal the prospective bride and bridegroom are not supposed to see each other again till that part of the wedding ceremony which is called *the Auspicious Vision*.

the fulness of his emotion a mist seemed to becloud his eyes.

At the gathering of women in the bridal chamber, after the wedding ceremony was over, an old village dame insisted that Kanti himself should take off his wife's bridal veil. As he did so he started back. It was not the same girl.

Something rose from within his breast and pierced into his brain. The light of the lamps seemed to grow dim, and darkness to tarnish the face of the bride herself.

At first he felt angry with his father-in-law. The old scoundrel had shown him one girl, and married him to another. But on calmer reflection he remembered that the old man had not shown him any daughter at all—that it was all his own fault. He thought it best not to show his arrant folly to the world, and took his place again with apparent calmness.

He could swallow the powder; he could not get rid of its taste. He could not bear the merry-makings of the festive throng. He was in a blaze of anger with himself as well as with everybody else.

Suddenly he felt the bride, seated by his side, give a little start and a suppressed scream; a leveret, scampering into the room, had brushed across her feet. Close upon it followed the girl he had seen before. She caught up the leveret into her arms, and began to caress it with an affectionate murmuring. 'Oh, the mad girl!' cried the women as they made signs to her to leave the room. She heeded them not, however, but came and unconcernedly sat in front of the wedded pair, looking into their faces with a childish curiosity. When a maidservant came and took her by the arm to lead her away, Kanti hurriedly interposed, saying, 'Let her be.'

'What is your name?' he then went on to ask her.

The girl swayed backwards and forwards but gave no reply. All the women in the room began to titter.

Kanti put another question: 'Have those ducklings of yours grown up?'

The girl stared at him as unconcernedly as before.

The bewildered Kanti screwed up courage for another effort, and asked tenderly after the wounded dove, but with no avail. The increasing laughter in the room betokened an amusing joke.

At last Kanti learned that the girl was deaf

and dumb, the companion of all the animals and birds of the locality. It was but by chance that she rose the other day when the name of Sudha was called.

Kanti now received a second shock. A black screen lifted from before his eyes. With a sigh of intense relief, as of escape from calamity, he looked once more into the face of his bride. Then came the true Auspicious Vision. The light from his heart and from the smokeless lamps fell on her gracious face ; and he saw it in its true radiance, knowing that Nabin's blessing would find fulfilment.

THE SUPREME NIGHT

THE SUPREME NIGHT

I USED to go to the same dame's school with Surabala and play at marriage with her. When I paid visits to her house, her mother would pet me, and setting us side by side would say to herself : ' What a lovely pair ! '

I was a child then, but I could understand her meaning well enough. The idea became rooted in my mind that I had a special right to Surabala above that of people in general. So it happened that, in the pride of ownership, at times I punished and tormented her ; and she, too, fagged for me and bore all my punishments without complaint. The village was wont to praise her beauty ; but in the eyes of a young barbarian like me that beauty had no glory ;—I knew only that Surabala had been born in her father's house solely to bear my yoke, and that therefore she was the particular object of my neglect.

My father was the land-steward of the Chaudhuris, a family of *zemindars*.   It was his plan, as soon as I had learnt to write a good hand, to train me in the work of estate management and secure a rent collectorship for me somewhere. But in my heart I disliked the proposal.   Nilratan of our village had run away to Calcutta, had learnt English there, and finally became the *Nazir*[1] of the District Magistrate ;   *that* was my life's ideal : I was secretly determined to be the Head Clerk of the Judge's Court, even if I could not become the Magistrate's *Nazir*.

I saw that my father always treated these court officers with the greatest respect.   I knew from my childhood that they had to be propitiated with gifts of fish, vegetables, and even money.   For this reason I had given a seat of high honour in my heart to the court underlings, even to the bailiffs.   These are the gods worshipped in our Bengal,—a modern miniature edition of the 330 millions of deities of the Hindu pantheon.   For gaining material success, people have more genuine faith in *them* than in the good Ganesh, the giver of success ; hence the people now offer to these officers everything that was formerly Ganesh's due.

---

[1] Superintendent of bailiffs.

Fired by the example of Nilratan, I too seized a suitable opportunity and ran away to Calcutta. There I first put up in the house of a village acquaintance, and afterwards got some funds from my father for my education.   Thus I carried on my studies regularly.

In addition, I joined political and benevolent societies.   I had no doubt whatever that it was urgently necessary for me to give my life suddenly for my country.   But I knew not how such a hard task could be carried out.   Also no one showed me the way.

But, nevertheless, my enthusiasm did not abate at all.   We country lads had not learnt to sneer at everything like the precocious boys of Calcutta, and hence our faith was very strong.   The 'leaders' of our associations delivered speeches, and we went begging for subscriptions from door to door in the hot blaze of noon without breaking our fast ; or we stood by the roadside distributing hand-bills, or arranged the chairs and benches in the lecture-hall, and, if anybody whispered a word against our leader, we got ready to fight him. For these things the city boys used to laugh at us as provincials.

I had come to Calcutta to be a *Nazir* or a

Head Clerk, but I was preparing to become a Mazzini or a Garibaldi.

At this time Surabala's father and my father laid their heads together to unite us in marriage. I had come to Calcutta at the age of fifteen; Surabala was eight years old then. I was now eighteen, and in my father's opinion I was almost past the age of marriage. But it was my secret vow to remain unmarried all my life and to die for my country; so I told my father that I would not marry before I had finished my education.

In two or three months I learnt that Surabala had been married to a pleader named Ram Lochan. I was then busy collecting subscriptions for raising fallen India, and this news did not seem worth my thought.

I had matriculated, and was about to appear at the Intermediate Examination, when my father died. I was not alone in the world, but had to maintain my mother and two sisters. I had therefore to leave college and look out for employment. After a good deal of exertion I secured the post of second master in the matriculation school of a small town in the Noakhali District.

I thought, here is just the work for me! By

my advice and inspiration I shall train up every
one of my pupils as a general for future India.

I began to work, and then found that the im-
pending examination was a more pressing affair
than the future of India. The headmaster got
angry whenever I talked of anything outside
grammar or algebra. And in a few months my
enthusiasm, too, flagged.

I am no genius. In the quiet of the home I
may form vast plans ; but when I enter the field of
work, I have to bear the yoke of the plough on
my neck like the Indian bullock, get my tail
twisted by my master, break clods all day, patiently
and with bowed head, and then at sunset have to
be satisfied if I can get any cud to chew. Such a
creature has not the spirit to prance and caper.

One of the teachers lived in the school-house, to
guard against fires. As I was a bachelor, this work
was thrown on me. I lodged in a thatched shed
close to the large cottage in which the school sat.

The school-house stood at some distance from
the inhabited portion of the town, and beside a
big tank. Around it were betel-nut, cocoa-nut,
and *madar* trees, and very near to the school
building two large ancient *nim* trees grew close
together, and cast a cool shade around.

F

One thing I have forgotten to mention, and indeed I had not so long considered it worth mentioning. The local Government pleader, Ram Lochan Ray, lived near our school. I also knew that his wife—my early playmate, Surabala—lived with him.

I got acquainted with Ram Lochan Babu. I cannot say whether he knew that I had known Surabala in childhood. I did not think fit to mention the fact at my first introduction to him. Indeed, I did not clearly remember that Surabala had been ever linked with my life in any way.

One holiday I paid a visit to Ram Lochan Babu. The subject of our conversation has gone out of my mind ; probably it was the unhappy condition of present-day India. Not that he was very much concerned or heart-broken over the matter ; but the subject was such that one could freely pour forth one's sentimental sorrow over it for an hour or two while puffing at one's *hooka*.

While thus engaged, I heard in a side-room the softest possible jingle of bracelets, crackle of dress, and footfall ; and I felt certain that two curious eyes were watching me through a small opening of the window.

All at once there flashed upon my memory a

pair of eyes,—a pair of large eyes, beaming with trust, simplicity, and girlhood's love,—black pupils, —thick dark eyelashes, — a calm fixed gaze. Suddenly some unseen force squeezed my heart in an iron grip, and it throbbed with intense pain.

I returned to my house, but the pain clung to me. Whether I read, wrote, or did any other work, I could not shake that weight off my heart ; a heavy load seemed to be always swinging from my heart-strings.

In the evening, calming myself a little, I began to reflect : ' What ails me ? ' From within came the question : ' Where is *your* Surabala now ? ' I replied : ' I gave her up of my free will. Surely I did not expect her to wait for me for ever.'

But something kept saying : ' *Then* you could have got her merely for the asking. *Now* you have not the right to look at her even once, do what you will. That Surabala of your boyhood may come very close to you ; you may hear the jingle of her bracelets ; you may breathe the air embalmed by the essence of her hair,—but there will always be a wall between you two.'

I answered : ' Be it so. What is Surabala to me ? '

My heart rejoined : ' To-day Surabala is nobody

to you.   But what might she not have been to
you ? '

Ah ! that's true.   *What* might she not have
been to me ?   Dearest to me of all things, closer
to me than the world besides, the sharer of all my
life's joys and sorrows,—she might have been.
And now, she is so distant, so much of a stranger,
that to look on her is forbidden, to talk with her
is improper, and to think of her is a sin !—while
this Ram Lochan, coming suddenly from nowhere,
has muttered a few set religious texts, and in one
swoop has carried off Surabala from the rest of
mankind !

I have not come to preach a new ethical code,
or to revolutionise society ; I have no wish to
tear asunder domestic ties.   I am only expressing
the exact working of my mind, though it may
not be reasonable.   I could not by any means
banish from my mind the sense that Surabala,
reigning there within shelter of Ram Lochan's
home, was mine far more than his.   The thought
was, I admit, unreasonable and improper,—but it
was not unnatural.

Thereafter I could not set my mind to any
kind of work.   At noon when the boys in my
class hummed, when Nature outside simmered in

the sun, when the sweet scent of the *nim* blossoms entered the room on the tepid breeze, I then wished,—I know not what I wished for ; but this I can say, that I did not wish to pass all my life in correcting the grammar exercises of those future hopes of India.

When school was over, I could not bear to live in my large lonely house ; and yet, if any one paid me a visit, it bored me. In the gloaming as I sat by the tank and listened to the meaningless breeze sighing through the betel- and cocoa-nut palms, I used to muse that human society is a web of mistakes ; nobody has the sense to do the right thing at the right time, and when the chance is gone we break our hearts over vain longings.

I could have married Surabala and lived happily. But I must be a Garibaldi,—and I ended by becoming the second master of a village school ! And pleader Ram Lochan Ray, who had no special call to be Surabala's husband,—to whom, before his marriage, Surabala was no wise different from a hundred other maidens,—has very quietly married her, and is earning lots of money as Government pleader ; when his dinner is badly cooked he scolds Surabala, and when he is in good humour he gives her a bangle ! He is sleek and

fat, tidily dressed, free from every kind of worry ;
he never passes his evenings by the tank gazing at
the stars and sighing.

Ram Lochan was called away from our town
for a few days by a big case elsewhere.   Surabala
in her house was as lonely as I was in my school
building.

I remember it was a Monday.   The sky was
overcast with clouds from the morning.   It began
to drizzle at ten o'clock.   At the aspect of the
heavens our headmaster closed the school early.
All day the black detached clouds began to run
about in the sky as if making ready for some grand
display.   Next day, towards afternoon, the rain
descended in torrents, accompanied by storm.
As the night advanced the fury of wind and
water increased.   At first the wind was easterly;
gradually it veered, and blew towards the south
and south-west.

It was idle to try to sleep on such a night.   I
remembered that in this terrible weather Surabala
was alone in her house.   Our school was much
more strongly built than her bungalow.   Often and
often did I plan to invite her to the school-house,
while I meant to pass the night alone by the tank.
But I could not summon up courage for it.

When it was half-past one in the morning, the roar of the tidal wave was suddenly heard,—the sea was rushing on us! I left my room and ran towards Surabala's house. In the way stood one embankment of our tank, and as I was wading to it the flood already reached my knees. When I mounted the bank, a second wave broke on it. The highest part of the bank was more than seventeen feet above the plain.

As I climbed up the bank, another person reached it from the opposite side. Who she was, every fibre of my body knew at once, and my whole soul was thrilled with the consciousness. I had no doubt that she, too, had recognised me.

On an island some three yards in area stood we two ; all else was covered with water.

It was a time of cataclysm ; the stars had been blotted out of the sky ; all the lights of the earth had been darkened ; there would have been no harm if we had held converse *then*. But we could not bring ourselves to utter a word ; neither of us made even a formal inquiry after the other's health. Only we stood gazing at the darkness. At our feet swirled the dense, black, wild, roaring torrent of death.

To-day Surabala has come to *my* side, leaving

the whole world.   To-day she has none besides *me*.
In our far-off childhood this Surabala had come
from some dark primeval realm of mystery, from a
life in another orb, and stood by my side on this
luminous peopled earth ; and to-day, after a wide
span of time, she has left that earth, so full of
light and human beings, to stand alone by *my* side
amidst this terrible desolate gloom of Nature's
death-convulsion.   The stream of birth had flung
that tender bud before me, and the flood of death
had wafted the same flower, now in full bloom, to
me and to none else.   One more wave and we shall
be swept away from this extreme point of the earth,
torn from the stalks on which we now sit apart,
and made one in death.

May that wave never come !   May Surabala
live long and happily, girt round by husband and
children, household and kinsfolk !   This one
night, standing on the brink of Nature's de-
struction, I have tasted eternal bliss.

The night wore out, the tempest ceased, the
flood abated ; without a word spoken, Surabala
went back to her house, and I, too, returned to
my shed without having uttered a word.

I reflected : True, I have become no *Nazir* or
Head Clerk, nor a Garibaldi ; I am only the second

master of a beggarly school.   But one night had
for its brief space beamed upon my whole life's
course.

That one night, out of all the days and nights
of my allotted span, has been the supreme glory of
my humble existence.

RAJA AND RANI

RAJA AND RANI

Bipin Kisore was born 'with a golden spoon in his mouth'; hence he knew how to squander money twice as well as how to earn it. The natural result was that he could not live long in the house where he was born.

He was a delicate young man of comely appearance, an adept in music, a fool in business, and unfit for life's handicap. He rolled along life's road like the wheel of Jagannath's car. He could not long command his wonted style of magnificent living.

Luckily, however, Raja Chittaranjan, having got back his property from the Court of Wards, was intent upon organising an Amateur Theatre Party. Captivated by the prepossessing looks of Bipin Kisore and his musical endowments, the Raja gladly 'admitted him of his crew.'

Chittaranjan was a B.A. He was not given to any excesses. Though the son of a rich man,

he used to dine and sleep at appointed hours
and even at appointed places.   And he suddenly
became enamoured of Bipin like one unto drink.
Often did meals cool and nights grow old while
he listened to Bipin and discussed with him the
merits of operatic compositions.   The Dewan
remarked that the only blemish in the otherwise
perfect character of his master was his inordinate
fondness for Bipin Kisore.

Rani Basanta Kumari raved at her husband,
and said that he was wasting himself on a luckless
baboon.   The sooner she could do away with him,
the easier she would feel.

The Raja was much pleased in his heart at this
seeming jealousy of his youthful wife.   He smiled,
and thought that women - folk know only one
man upon the earth—him whom they love ; and
never think of other men's deserts.   That there
may be many whose merits deserve regard, is not
recorded in the scriptures of women.   The only
good man and the only object of a woman's favours
is he who has blabbered into her ears the matri-
monial incantations.   A little moment behind the
usual hour of her husband's meals is a world of
anxiety to her, but she never cares a brass button
if her husband's dependents have a mouthful or

not. This inconsiderate partiality of the softer sex might be cavilled at, but to Chittaranjan it did not seem unpleasant. Thus, he would often indulge in hyperbolic laudations of Bipin in his wife's presence, just to provoke a display of her delightful fulminations.

But what was sport to the 'royal' couple, was death to poor Bipin. The servants of the house, as is their wont, took their cue from the Rani's apathetic and wilful neglect of the wretched hanger-on, and grew more apathetic and wilful still. They contrived to forget to look after his comforts, to Bipin's infinite chagrin and untold sufferings.

Once the Rani rebuked the servant Puté, and said : ' You are always shirking work ; what do you do all through the day ? ' ' Pray, madam, the whole day is taken up in serving Bipin Babu under the Maharaja's orders,' stammered the poor valet.

The Rani retorted : 'Your Bipin Babu is a great Nawab, eh ? ' This was enough for Puté. He took the hint. From the very next day he left Bipin Babu's orts as they were, and at times forgot to cover the food for him. With unpractised hands Bipin often scoured his own dishes and not

unfrequently went without meals.   But it was not
in him to whine and report to the Raja.   It was
not in him to lower himself by petty squabblings
with menials.   He did not mind it ; he took
everything in good part.   And thus while the
Raja's favours grew, the Rani's disfavour in-
tensified, and at last knew no bounds.

Now the opera of *Subhadraharan* was ready
after due rehearsal.   The stage was fitted up in
the palace court-yard.   The Raja acted the part
of ' Krishna,' and Bipin that of ' Arjuna.'   Oh,
how sweetly he sang ! how beautiful he looked !
The audience applauded in transports of joy.

The play over, the Raja came to the Rani and
asked her how she liked it.   The Rani replied :
' Indeed, Bipin acted the part of " Arjuna " glori-
ously ! He does look like the scion of a noble
family.   His voice is rare ! '   The Raja said
jocosely : ' And how do I look ?   Am I not fair ?
Have I not a sweet voice ? '   ' Oh, yours is a
different case ! ' added the Rani, and again fell to
dilating on the histrionic abilities of Bipin Kisore.

The tables were now turned.   He who used
to praise, now began to deprecate.   The Raja, who
was never weary of indulging in high-sounding
panegyrics of Bipin before his consort, now

suddenly fell reflecting that, after all, unthinking
people made too much of Bipin's actual merits.
What was extraordinary about his appearance or
voice? A short while before he himself was
one of those unthinking men, but in a sudden
and mysterious way he developed symptoms of
thoughtfulness !

From the day following, every good arrange-
ment was made for Bipin's meals. The Rani told
the Raja : ' It is undoubtedly wrong to lodge
Bipin Babu with the petty officers of the Raj in
the Kachari[1]; for all he now is, he was once a man
of means.' The Raja ejaculated curtly : ' Ha ! '
and turned the subject. The Rani proposed that
there might be another performance on the occasion
of the first-rice ceremony of the ' royal ' weanling.
The Raja heard and heard her not.

Once on being reprimanded by the Raja for
not properly laying his cloth, the servant Puté
replied : ' What can I do? According to the
Rani's behests I have to look after Bipin Babu and
wait on him the livelong day.' This angered the
Raja, and he exclaimed, highly nettled : ' Pshaw !
Bipin Babu is a veritable Nawab, I see ! Can't he
cleanse his own dishes himself ? ' The servant, as

---

[1] *Kachari*, generally anglicised as *cuteberry* : offices and courts.

before, took his cue, and Bipin lapsed back into his former wretchedness.

The Rani liked Bipin's songs—they were sweet —there was no gainsaying it. When her husband sat with Bipin to the wonted discourses of sweet music of an evening, she would listen from behind the screen in an adjoining room. Not long afterwards, the Raja began again his old habit of dining and sleeping at regular hours. The music came to an end. Bipin's evening services were no more needed.

Raja Chittaranjan used to look after his *zemindari* affairs at noon. One day he came earlier to the zenana, and found his consort reading something. On his asking her what she read, the Rani was a little taken aback, but promptly replied : ' I am conning over a few songs from Bipin Babu's song-book. We have not had any music since you tired abruptly of your musical hobby.' Poor woman ! it was she who had herself made no end of efforts to eradicate the hobby from her husband's mind.

On the morrow the Raja dismissed Bipin— without a thought as to how and where the poor fellow would get a morsel henceforth !

Nor was this the only matter of regret to

Bipin.   He had been bound to the Raja by the
dearest and most sincere tie of attachment.   He
served him more for affection than for pay.   He
was fonder of his friend than of the wages he
received.   Even after deep cogitation, Bipin could
not ascertain the cause of the Raja's sudden
estrangement.   ''Tis Fate ! all is Fate ! ' Bipin
said to himself.   And then, silently and bravely,
he heaved a deep sigh, picked up his old guitar,
put it up in the case, paid the last two coins in his
pocket as a farewell *bakshish* to Puté, and walked
out into the wide wide world where he had not a
soul to call his friend.

THE TRUST PROPERTY

THE TRUST PROPERTY

BRINDABAN KUNDU came to his father in a rage
and said : ' I am off this moment.'

' Ungrateful wretch ! ' sneered the father,
Jaganath Kundu. ' When you have paid me
back all that I have spent on your food and clothing, it will be time enough to give yourself these
airs.'

Such food and clothing as was customary in
Jaganath's household could not have cost very
much. Our *rishis* of old managed to feed and
clothe themselves on an incredibly small outlay.
Jaganath's behaviour showed that his ideal in these
respects was equally high. That he could not
fully live up to it was due partly to the bad influence of the degenerate society around him, and
partly to certain unreasonable demands of Nature
in her attempt to keep body and soul together.

So long as Brindaban was single, things went

smoothly enough, but after his marriage he began to depart from the high and rarefied standard cherished by his sire.   It was clear that the son's ideas of comfort were moving away from the spiritual to the material, and imitating the ways of the world.   He was unwilling to put up with the discomforts of heat and cold, thirst and hunger.   His minimum of food and clothing rose apace.

Frequent were the quarrels between the father and the son.   At last Brindaban's wife became seriously ill and a *kabiraj*[1] was called in.   But when the doctor prescribed a costly medicine for his patient, Jaganath took it as a proof of sheer incompetence, and turned him out immediately. At first Brindaban besought his father to allow the treatment to continue ; then he quarrelled with him about it, but to no purpose.   When his wife died, he abused his father and called him a murderer.

'Nonsense !' said the father.   'Don't people die even after swallowing all kinds of drugs ?   If costly medicines could save life, how is it that kings and emperors are not immortal ?   You don't expect your wife to die with more pomp and

---

[1] Country doctor, unqualified by any medical training.

ceremony than did your mother and your grand-mother before her, do you ? '

Brindaban might really have derived a great consolation from these words, had he not been overwhelmed with grief and incapable of proper thinking.   Neither his mother nor his grand-mother had taken any medicine before making their exit from this world, and this was the time-honoured custom of the family.   But, alas, the younger generation was unwilling to die according to ancient custom.   The English had newly come to the country at the time we speak of.   Even in those remote days, the good old folks were horri-fied at the unorthodox ways of the new generation, and sat speechless, trying to draw comfort from their *hookas*.

Be that as it may, the modern Brindaban said to his old fogy of a father : ' I am off.'

The father instantly agreed, and wished publicly that, should he ever give his son one single pice in future, the gods might reckon his act as shedding the holy blood of cows.   Brindaban in his turn similarly wished that, should he ever accept any-thing from his father, his act might be held as bad as matricide.

The people of the village looked upon this

small revolution as a great relief after a long period
of monotony.   And when Jaganath disinherited
his only son, every one did his best to console him.
All were unanimous in the opinion that to quarrel
with a father for the sake of a wife was possible
only in these degenerate days.   And the reason
they gave was sound too.   ' When your wife dies,'
they said, ' you can find a second one without delay.
But when your father dies, you can't get another
to replace him for love or money.'   Their logic
no doubt was perfect, but we suspect that the
utter hopelessness of getting another father did
not trouble the misguided son very much.   On
the contrary, he looked upon it as a mercy.

Nor did separation from Brindaban weigh
heavily on the mind of his father.   In the first
place, his absence from home reduced the household expenses.   Then, again, the father was freed
from a great anxiety.   The fear of being poisoned
by his son and heir had always haunted him.
When he ate his scanty fare, he could never banish
the thought of poison from his mind.   This fear
had abated somewhat after the death of his
daughter-in-law, and, now that the son was gone,
it disappeared altogether.

But there was one tender spot in the old man's

heart. Brindaban had taken away with him his four-year-old son, Gokul Chandra. Now, the expense of keeping the child was comparatively small, and so Jaganath's affection for him was without a drawback. Still, when Brindaban took him away, his grief, sincere as it was, was mingled at first with calculation as to how much he would save a month by the absence of the two, how much the sum would come to in the year, and what would be the capital to bring it in as interest.

But the empty house, without Gokul Chandra in it to make mischief, became more and more difficult for the old man to live in. There was no one now to play tricks upon him when he was engaged in his *puja*,[1] no one to snatch away his food and eat it, no one to run away with his ink-pot, when he was writing up his accounts. His daily routine of life, now uninterrupted, became an intolerable burden to him. He bethought him that this unworried peace was endurable only in the world to come. When he caught sight of the holes made in his quilt by his grandchild, and the pen-and-ink sketches executed by the same artist on his rush-mat, his heart was heavy with grief. Once upon a time he had reproached the boy

[1] A ceremonial worship.

bitterly because he had torn his *dhoti* into pieces within the short space of two years ; now tears stood in Jaganath's eyes as he gazed upon the dirty remnants lying in the bedroom. He carefully put them away in his safe, and registered a vow that, should Gokul ever come back again, he should not be reprimanded even if he destroyed one *dhoti* a year.

But Gokul did not return, and poor Jaganath aged rapidly. His empty home seemed emptier every day.

No longer could the old man stay peacefully at home. Even in the middle of the day, when all respectable folks in the village enjoyed their after-dinner siesta, Jaganath might be seen roaming over the village, *hooka* in hand. The boys, at sight of him, would give up their play, and, retiring in a body to a safe distance, chant verses composed by a local poet, praising the old gentleman's economical habits. No one ventured to say his real name, lest he should have to go without his meal that day [1]—and so people gave him names after their own fancy. Elderly people called him Jaganash, [2]

---

[1] It is a superstition current in Bengal that if a man pronounces the name of a very miserly individual, he has to go without his meal that day.

[2] Jaganath is the Lord of Festivity, and Jaga*nash* would mean the despoiler of it.

but the reason why the younger generation pre-
ferred to call him a vampire was hard to guess.
It may be that the bloodless, dried-up skin of the
old man had some physical resemblance to the
vampire's.

II

One afternoon, when Jaganath was rambling as
usual through the village lanes shaded by mango
topes, he saw a boy, apparently a stranger, assuming
the captaincy of the village boys and explaining to
them the scheme of some new prank. Won by
the force of his character and the startling novelty
of his ideas, the boys had all sworn allegiance to
him. Unlike the others, he did not run away
from the old man as he approached, but came
quite close to him and began to shake his own
chadar. The result was that a live lizard sprang
out of it on to the old man's body, ran down his
back and off towards the jungle. Sudden fright
made the poor man shiver from head to foot, to
the great amusement of the other boys, who shouted
with glee. Before Jaganath had gone far, cursing
and swearing, the *gamcha* on his shoulder suddenly
disappeared, and the next moment it was seen on
the head of the new boy, transformed into a
turban.

The novel attentions of this manikin came as a great relief to Jaganath. It was long since any boy had taken such freedom with him. After a good deal of coaxing and many fair promises, he at last persuaded the boy to come to him, and this was the conversation which followed :

' What's your name, my boy ? '

' Nitai Pal.'

' Where's your home ? '

' Won't tell.'

' Who's your father ? '

' Won't tell.'

' Why won't you ? '

' Because I have run away from home.'

' What made you do it ? '

' My father wanted to send me to school.'

It occurred to Jaganath that it would be useless extravagance to send such a boy to school, and his father must have been an unpractical fool not to have thought so.

' Well, well,' said Jaganath, ' how would you like to come and stay with me ? '

' Don't mind,' said the boy, and forthwith he installed himself in Jaganath's house. He felt as little hesitation as though it were the shadow of a tree by the wayside. And not only that. He

began to proclaim his wishes as regards his food
and clothing with such coolness that you would
have thought he had paid his reckoning in full
beforehand ; and, when anything went wrong, he
did not scruple to quarrel with the old man.   It
had been easy enough for Jaganath to get the better
of his own child ; but, now, where another man's
child was concerned, he had to acknowledge defeat.

III

The people of the village marvelled when
Nitai Pal was unexpectedly made so much of by
Jaganath.   They felt sure that the old man's end
was near, and the prospect of his bequeathing all
his property to this unknown brat made their
hearts sore.   Furious with envy, they determined
to do the boy an injury, but the old man took care
of him as though he was a rib in his breast.

At times, the boy threatened that he would go
away, and the old man used to say to him tempt-
ingly : ' I will leave you all the property I possess.'
Young as he was, the boy fully understood the
grandeur of this promise.

The village people then began to make inquiries
after the father of the boy.   Their hearts melted
with compassion for the agonised parents, and they

declared that the son must be a rascal to cause them so much suffering. They heaped abuses on his head, but the heat with which they did it betrayed envy rather than a sense of justice.

One day the old man learned from a wayfarer that one Damodar Pal was seeking his lost son, and was even now coming towards the village. Nitai, when he heard this, became very restless and was ready to run away, leaving his future wealth to take care of itself. Jaganath reassured him, saying : 'I mean to hide you where nobody can find you — not even the village people themselves.'

This whetted the curiosity of the boy and he said : 'Oh, where ?　Do show me.'

'People will know, if I show you now.　Wait till it is night,' said Jaganath.

The hope of discovering the mysterious hiding-place delighted Nitai.　He planned to himself how, as soon as his father had gone away without him, he would have a bet with his comrades, and play hide-and-seek.　Nobody would be able to find him.　Wouldn't it be fun ?　His father, too, would ransack the whole village, and not find him—that would be rare fun also.

At noon, Jaganath shut the boy up in his house,

and disappeared for some time. When he came home again, Nitai worried him with questions.

No sooner was it dark than Nitai said : ' Grandfather, shall we go now ? '

' It isn't night yet,' replied Jaganath.

A little while later the boy exclaimed : ' It is night now, grandfather ; come let's go.'

' The village people haven't gone to bed yet,' whispered Jaganath.

Nitai waited but a moment, and said : ' They have gone to bed now, grandfather ; I am sure they have. Let's start now.'

The night advanced. Sleep began to weigh heavily on the eyelids of the poor boy, and it was a hard struggle for him to keep awake. At midnight, Jaganath caught hold of the boy's arm, and left the house, groping through the dark lanes of the sleeping village. Not a sound disturbed the stillness, except the occasional howl of a dog, when all the other dogs far and near would join in chorus, or perhaps the flapping of a night-bird, scared by the sound of human footsteps at that unusual hour. Nitai trembled with fear, and held Jaganath fast by the arm.

Across many a field they went, and at last came to a jungle, where stood a dilapidated temple

H

without a god in it. 'What, here!' exclaimed
Nitai in a tone of disappointment. It was nothing
like what he had imagined. There was not much
mystery about it. Often, since running away from
home, he had passed nights in deserted temples like
this. It was not a bad place for playing hide-and-
seek ; still it was quite possible that his comrades
might track him there.

From the middle of the floor inside, Jaganath
removed a slab of stone, and an underground room
with a lamp burning in it was revealed to the
astonished eyes of the boy. Fear and curiosity
assailed his little heart. Jaganath descended by a
ladder and Nitai followed him.

Looking around, the boy saw that there were
brass *ghurras* [1] on all sides of him. In the middle
lay spread an *assan*,[2] and in front of it were
arranged vermilion, sandal paste, flowers, and other
articles of *puja*. To satisfy his curiosity the boy
dipped his hand into some of the *ghurras*, and
drew out their contents. They were rupees and
gold *mohurs*.

Jaganath, addressing the boy, said : 'I told you,
Nitai, that I would give you all my money. I

---

[1] A water-pot holding about three gallons of water.
[2] A prayer carpet.

have not got much,—these *ghurras* are all that I possess. These I will make over to you to-day.'

The boy jumped with delight. ' All? ' he exclaimed ; 'you won't take back a rupee, will you ? '

' If I do,' said the old man in solemn tones, ' may my hand be attacked with leprosy. But there is one condition. If ever my grandson, Gokul Chandra, or his son, or his grandson, or his great-grandson or any of his progeny should happen to pass this way, then you must make over to him, or to them, every rupee and every *mohur* here.'

The boy thought that the old man was raving. ' Very well,' he replied.

' Then sit on this *assan*,' said Jaganath.

' What for ? '

' Because *puja* will be done to you.'

' But why ? ' said the boy, taken aback

' This is the rule.'

The boy squatted on the *assan* as he was told. Jaganath smeared his forehead with sandal paste, put a mark of vermilion between his eyebrows, flung a garland of flowers round his neck, and began to recite *mantras*.[1]

---

[1] Incantations.

To sit there like a god, and hear *mantras* recited made poor Nitai feel very uneasy. ' Grandfather,' he whispered.

But Jaganath did not reply, and went on muttering his incantations.

Finally, with great difficulty he dragged each *ghurra* before the boy and made him repeat the following vow after him :

' I do solemnly promise that I will make over all this treasure to Gokul Chandra Kundu, the son of Brindaban Kundu, the grandson of Jaganath Kundu, or to the son or to the grandson or to the great‑grandson of the said Gokul Chandra Kundu, or to any other progeny of his who may be the rightful heir.'

The boy repeated this over and over again, until he felt stupefied, and his tongue began to grow stiff in his mouth. When the ceremony was over, the air of the cave was laden with the smoke of the earthen lamp and the breath-poison of the two. The boy felt that the roof of his mouth had become dry as dust, and his hands and feet were burning. He was nearly suffocated.

The lamp became dimmer and dimmer, and then went out altogether. In the total darkness that followed, Nitai could hear the old man climb‑

ing up the ladder. 'Grandfather, where are you going to ?' said he, greatly distressed.

'I am going now,' replied Jaganath; 'you remain here. No one will be able to find you. Remember the name Gokul Chandra, the son of Brindaban, and the grandson of Jaganath.'

He then withdrew the ladder. In a stifled, agonised voice the boy implored : 'I want to go back to father.'

Jaganath replaced the slab. He then knelt down and placed his ear on the stone. Nitai's voice was heard once more—'Father'—and then came a sound of some heavy object falling with a bump—and then—everything was still.

Having thus placed his wealth in the hands of a *yak*,[1] Jaganath began to cover up the stone with earth. Then he piled broken bricks and loose mortar over it. On the top of all he planted turfs of grass and jungle weeds. The night was almost spent, but he could not tear himself away from the spot. Now and again he placed his ear to the ground, and tried to listen. It seemed to him that from far far below—from the abysmal depth of the earth's interior—came a wailing. It seemed to

[1] *Yak* or *Yaksa* is a supernatural being described in Sanskrit mythology and poetry. In Bengal, *Yak* has come to mean a ghostly custodian of treasure, under such circumstances as in this story.

him that the night-sky was flooded with that one sound, that the sleeping humanity of all the world was awake, and was sitting on its beds, trying to listen.

The old man in his frenzy kept on heaping earth higher and higher. He wanted somehow to stifle that sound, but still he fancied he could hear ' Father.'

He struck the spot with all his might and said : ' Be quiet—people might hear you.' But still he imagined he heard ' Father.'

The sun lighted up the eastern horizon. Jaganath then left the temple, and came into the open fields.

There, too, somebody called out ' Father.' Startled at the sound, he turned back and saw his son at his heels.

' Father,' said Brindaban, ' I hear my boy is hiding himself in your house. I must have him back.'

With eyes dilated and distorted mouth, the old man leaned forward and exclaimed : ' Your boy ? '

' Yes, my boy Gokul. He is Nitai Pal now, and I myself go by the name of Damodar Pal. Your *fame* has spread so widely in the neighbourhood, that we were obliged to cover up our origin, lest people should have refused to pronounce our names.'

Slowly the old man lifted both his arms above his head. His fingers began to twitch convulsively, as though he was trying to catch hold of some imaginary object in the air. He then fell on the ground.

When he came to his senses again, he dragged his son towards the ruined temple. When they were both inside it, he said : ' Do you hear any wailing sound ? '

' No, I don't,' said Brindaban.

' Just listen very carefully. Do you hear anybody calling out " Father " ? '

' No.'

This seemed to relieve him greatly.

From that day forward, he used to go about asking people : ' Do you hear any wailing sound ? ' They laughed at the raving dotard.

About four years later, Jaganath lay on his death-bed. When the light of this world was gradually fading away from his eyes, and his breathing became more and more difficult, he suddenly sat up in a state of delirium. Throwing both his hands in the air he seemed to grope about for something, muttering : ' Nitai, who has removed my ladder ? '

Unable to find the ladder to climb out of his terrible dungeon, where there was no light to see and no air to breathe, he fell on his bed once more, and disappeared into that region where no one has ever been found out in the world's eternal game of hide-and-seek.[1]

---

[1] The incidents described in this story, now happily a thing of the past, were by no means rare in Bengal at one time. Our author, however, slightly departs from the current accounts. Such criminally superstitious practices were resorted to by miserly persons under the idea that they themselves would re-acquire the treasure in a future state of existence. 'When you see me in a future birth passing this way, you must make over all this treasure to me. Guard it till then and stir not,'—was the usual promise exacted from the victim before he became *yak*. Many were the 'true' stories we heard in childhood of people becoming suddenly rich by coming across ghostly custodians of wealth belonging to them in a past birth.

THE RIDDLE SOLVED

THE RIDDLE SOLVED

I

KRISHNA GOPAL SIRCAR, zemindar of Jhikrakota, made over his estates to his eldest son, and retired to Kasi, as befits a good Hindu, to spend the evening of his life in religious devotion. All the poor and the destitute of the neighbourhood were in tears at the parting. Every one declared that such piety and benevolence were rare in these degenerate days.

His son, Bipin Bihari, was a young man well educated after the modern fashion, and had taken the degree of Bachelor of Arts. He sported a pair of spectacles, wore a beard, and seldom mixed with others. His private life was unsullied. He did not smoke, and never touched cards. He was a man of stern disposition, though he looked soft and pliable. This trait of his character soon came home to his tenantry in diverse ways. Unlike his father, he would on no account allow the remission of one single pice out of the rents justly due to him. In no circumstances would he grant any tenant one single day's grace in paying up.

On taking over the management of the property, Bipin Bihari discovered that his father had allowed a large number of Brahmins to hold land entirely rent-free, and a larger number at rents much below the prevailing rates. His father was incapable of resisting the importunate solicitation of others—such was the weakness of his character.

Bipin Bihari said this could never be. He could not abandon the income of half his property —and he reasoned with himself thus : *Firstly*, the persons who were in actual enjoyment of the concessions and getting fat at his expense were a lot of worthless people, and wholly undeserving of charity. Charity bestowed on such objects only encouraged idleness. *Secondly*, living nowadays had become much costlier than in the days of his ancestors. Wants had increased apace. For a gentleman to keep up his position had become four times as expensive as in days past. So he could not afford to scatter gifts right and left as his father had done. On the contrary, it was his bounden duty to call back as many of them as he possibly could.

So Bipin Bihari lost no time in carrying into effect what he conceived to be his duty. He was a man of strict principles.

What had gone out of his grasp, returned to him little by little. Only a very small portion of his father's grants did he allow to remain undisturbed, and he took good care to arrange that even those should not be deemed permanent.

The wails of the tenants reached Krishna Gopal at Benares through the post. Some even made a journey to that place to represent their grievances to him in person. Krishna Gopal wrote to his son intimating his displeasure. Bipin Bihari replied, pointing out that the times had changed. In former days, he said, the *zemindar* was compensated for the gifts he made by the many customary presents he received from his tenantry. Recent statutes had made all such impositions illegal. The *zemindar* had now to rest content with just the stipulated rent, and nothing more. 'Unless,' he continued, 'we keep a strict watch over the payment of our just dues, what will be left to us ? Since the tenants won't give us anything extra now, how can we allow them concessions ? Our relations must henceforth be strictly commercial. We shall be ruined if we go on making gifts and endowments, and the preservation of our property and the keeping up of our position will be rendered very difficult.'

Krishna Gopal became uneasy at finding that times should have changed so much. 'Well, well,' he murmured to himself, 'the younger generation knows best, I suppose. Our old-fashioned methods won't do now. If I interfere, my son might refuse to manage the property, and insist on my going back. No, thank you—I would rather not. I prefer to devote the few days that are left me to the service of my God.'

II

So things went on. Bipin Bihari put his affairs in order after much litigation in the Courts, and by less constitutional methods outside. Most of the tenants submitted to his will out of fear. Only a fellow called Asimuddin, son of Mirza Bibi, remained refractory.

Bipin's displeasure was keenest against this man. He could quite understand his father having granted rent-free lands to Brahmins, but why this Mohammedan should be holding so much land, some free and some at rents lower than the prevailing rates, was a riddle to him. And what

was he ?   The son of a low Mohammedan widow,
giving himself airs and defying the whole world,
simply because he had learnt to read and write a
little at the village school.   To Bipin it was intolerable.

He made inquiries of his clerks about Asimuddin's holdings.   All that they could tell him was
that Babu Krishna Gopal himself had made these
grants to the family many years back, but they
had no idea as to what his motive might have
been.   They imagined, however, that perhaps the
widow won the compassion of the kind-hearted
zemindar, by representing to him her woe and
misery.

To Bipin these favours seemed to be utterly
undeserved.   He had not seen the pitiable condition of these people in days gone by.   Their
comparative ease at the present day and their
arrogance drove him to the conclusion that they
had impudently swindled his tender-hearted father
out of a part of his lawful income.

Asimuddin was a stiff-necked sort of a fellow,
too.   He vowed that he would lay down his life
sooner than give up an inch of his land.   Then
came open hostilities.

The poor old widow tried her best to pacify

her son. 'It is no good fighting with the *zemindar*,' she would often say to him. 'His kindness has kept us alive so long ; let us depend upon him still, though he may curtail his favours. Surrender to him part of the lands as he desires.'

'Oh, mother !' protested Asimuddin. 'What do you know of these matters, pray ? '

One by one, Asimuddin lost the cases instituted against him. The more he lost, the more his obstinacy increased. For the sake of his all, he staked all that was his.

One afternoon, Mirza Bibi collected some fruits and vegetables from her little garden, and unknown to her son went and sought an interview with Bipin Babu. She looked at him with a tenderness maternal in its intensity, and spoke : 'May Allah bless you, my son. Do not destroy Asim—it wouldn't be right of you. To your charge I commit him. Take him as though he were one whom it is your duty to support—as though he were a ne'er-do-well younger brother of yours. Vast is your wealth—don't grudge him a small particle of it, my son.'

This assumption of familiarity on the part of the garrulous old woman annoyed Bipin not a little. 'What do you know of these things, my good woman?' he condescended to say. 'If you have any representations to make, send your son to me.'

Being assured for the second time that she knew nothing about these affairs, Mirza Bibi returned home, wiping her eyes with her apron all the way, and offering her silent prayers to Allah.

III

The litigation dragged its weary length from the Criminal to the Civil Courts, and thence to the High Court, where at last Asimuddin met with a partial success. Eighteen months passed in this way. But he was a ruined man now—plunged in debts up to his very ears. His creditors took this opportunity to execute the decrees they had obtained against him. A date was fixed for putting up to auction every stick and stone that he had left.

It was Monday. The village market had assembled by the side of a tiny river, now swollen by the rains. Buying and selling were going on, partly on the bank and partly in the boats moored there. The hubbub was great. Among the commodities for sale jack-fruits preponderated, it being the month of *Asadh*. *Hilsa* fish were seen in large quantities also. The sky was cloudy.

Many of the stall-holders, apprehending a down-pour, had stretched a piece of cloth overhead, across bamboo poles put up for the purpose.

Asimuddin had come too—but he had not a copper with him. No shopkeepers allowed him credit nowadays. He therefore had brought a brass *thali*[1] and a *dao*[2] with him. These he would pawn, and then buy what he needed.

Towards evening, Bipin Babu was out for a walk attended by two or three retainers armed with *lathis*.[3] Attracted by the noise, he directed his steps towards the market. On his arrival, he stopped awhile before the stall of Dwari, the oil-man, and made kindly inquiries about his business. All on a sudden, Asimuddin raised his *dao* and ran towards Bipin Babu, roaring like a tiger. The market people caught hold of him half-way, and quickly disarmed him. He was forthwith given in custody to the police. Business in the market then went on as usual.

We cannot say that Bipin Babu was not in-wardly pleased at this incident. It is intolerable that the creature we are hunting down should turn and show fight. 'The *badmash*,' Bipin chuckled ; ' I have got him at last.'

---

[1] *Thali* : plate.   [2] *Dao* : knife.   [3] *Lathis* : stick.

The ladies of Bipin Babu's house, when they heard the news, exclaimed with horror : ' Oh, the ruffian !   What a mercy they seized him in time ! ' They found consolation in the prospect of the man being punished as he richly deserved.

In another part of the village the same evening the widow's humble cottage, devoid of bread and bereft of her son, became darker than death. Others dismissed the incident of the afternoon from their minds, sat down to their meals, retired to bed and went to sleep, but to the widow the event loomed larger than anything else in this wide world.   But, alas, who was there to combat it ? Only a bundle of wearied bones and a helpless mother's heart trembling with fear.

IV

Three days have passed in the meanwhile.   To-morrow the case would come up for trial before a Deputy Magistrate.   Bipin Babu would have to be examined as a witness.   Never before this did a *zemindar* of Jhikrakota appear in the witness-box, but Bipin did not mind.

The next day at the appointed hour, Bipin Babu arrived at the Court in a palanquin in great state. He wore a turban on his head, and a watch-chain dangled on his breast. The Deputy Magistrate invited him to a seat on the daïs, beside his own. The Court-room was crowded to suffocation. So great a sensation had not been witnessed in this Court for many years.

When the time for the case to be called drew near, a *chaprassi* came and whispered something in Bipin Babu's ear. He got up very agitated and walked out, begging the Deputy Magistrate to excuse him for a few minutes.

Outside he saw his old father a little way off, standing under a *banian* tree, barefooted and wrapped in a piece of *namabali*.[1] A string of beads was in his hand. His slender form shone with a gentle lustre, and tranquil compassion seemed to radiate from his forehead.

Bipin, hampered by his close-fitting trousers and his flowing *chapkan*, touched his father's feet with his forehead. As he did this his turban came off and kissed his nose, and his watch, popping out of his pocket, swung to and fro in the air. Bipin hurriedly straightened his turban, and begged his father to come to his pleader's house close by.

' No, thank you,' Krishna Gopal replied, ' I will tell you here what I have got to say.'

---

[1] A garment with the name of Krishna printed over it.

A curious crowd had gathered by this time. Bipin's attendants pushed them back.

Then Krishna Gopal said : ' You must do what you can to get Asim acquitted, and restore him the lands that you have taken away from him.'

' Is it for this, father,' said Bipin, very much surprised, ' that you have come all the way from Benares ?   Would you tell me why you have made these people the objects of your special favour ? '

' What would you gain by knowing it, my boy ? '

But Bipin persisted.   ' It is only this, father,' he went on ; ' I have revoked many a grant because I thought the tenants were not deserving.   There were many Brahmins among them, but of them you never said a word. Why are you so keen about these Mohammedans now ?   After all that has happened, if I drop this case against Asim, and give him back his lands, what shall I say to people ? '

Krishna Gopal kept silence for some moments. Then, passing the beads through his shaky fingers with rapidity, he spoke with a tremulous voice : ' Should it be necessary to explain your conduct to people, you may tell them that Asimuddin is my son—and your brother.'

' What ? ' exclaimed Bipin in painful surprise. ' From a Musalman's womb ? '

' Even so, my son,' was the calm reply.

Bipin stood there for some time in mute astonishment. Then he found words to say : 'Come home, father ; we will talk about it afterwards.'

' No, my son,' replied the old man, ' having once relinquished the world to serve my God, I cannot go home again. I return hence. Now I leave you to do what your sense of duty may suggest.' He then blessed his son, and, checking his tears with difficulty, walked off with tottering steps.

Bipin was dumbfounded, not knowing what to say nor what to do. ' So, such was the piety of the older generation,' he said to himself. He reflected with pride how much better he was than his father in point of education and morality. This was the result, he concluded, of not having a principle to guide one's actions.

Returning to the Court, he saw Asimuddin outside between two constables, awaiting his trial. He looked emaciated and worn out. His lips were pale and dry, and his eyes unnaturally bright. A dirty piece of cloth worn to shreds covered him. ' This my brother ! ' Bipin shuddered at the thought.

The Deputy Magistrate and Bipin were friends,

and the case ended in a fiasco.   In a few days Asimuddin was restored to his former condition. Why all this happened, he could not understand. The village people were greatly surprised also.

However, the news of Krishna Gopal's arrival just before the trial soon got abroad.   People began to exchange meaning glances.   The pleaders in their shrewdness guessed the whole affair.   One of them, Ram Taran Babu, was beholden to Krishna Gopal for his education and his start in life.   Somehow or other he had always suspected that the virtue and piety of his benefactor were shams.   Now he was fully convinced that, if a searching inquiry were made, all ' pious ' men might be found out. ' Let them tell their beads as much as they like,' he thought with glee, ' everybody in this world is just as bad as myself.   The only difference between a good and a bad man is that the good practise dissimulation while the bad don't.'   The revelation that Krishna Gopal's far-famed piety, benevolence, and magnanimity were nothing but a cloak of hypocrisy, settled a difficulty that had oppressed Ram Taran Babu for many years.   By what process of reasoning, we do not know, the burden of gratitude was greatly lifted off his mind.   It was a vast relief to him !

THE ELDER SISTER

THE ELDER SISTER

I

HAVING described at length the misdeeds of an unfortunate woman's wicked, tyrannical husband, Tara, the woman's neighbour in the village, very shortly declared her verdict : ' Fire be to such a husband's mouth.'

At this Joygopal Babu's wife felt much hurt ; it did not become womankind to wish, in any circumstances whatever, a worse species of fire than that of a cigar in a husband's mouth.

When, therefore, she mildly disapproved the verdict, hard-hearted Tara cried with redoubled vehemence : ' 'Twere better to be a widow seven births over than the wife of such a husband,' and saying this she broke up the meeting and left.

Sasi said within herself : ' I can't imagine any offence in a husband that could so harden the heart against him.' Even as she turned the matter over in her mind, all the tenderness of her loving soul gushed forth towards her own husband now abroad. Throwing herself with outstretched arms on that part of the bed whereon her husband was wont to lie, she kissed the empty pillow, caught the smell of her husband's head, and, shutting the door, brought out from a wooden box an old and almost faded photograph with some letters in his handwriting, and sat gazing upon them. Thus she passed the hushed noontide alone in her room, musing of old memories and shedding tears of sadness.

It was no new yoke this between Sasikala and Joygopal. They had been married at an early age and had children. Their long companionship had made the days go by in an easy, commonplace sort of way. On neither side had there been any symptoms of excessive passion. They had lived together nearly sixteen years without a break, when her husband was suddenly called away from home on business, and then a great impulse of love awoke in Sasi's soul. As separation strained the tie, love's knot grew tighter, and the passion, whose existence Sasi had not felt, now made her throb with pain.

So it happened that after so many long years,

and at such an age, and being the mother of children, Sasi, on this spring noon, in her lonely chamber, lying on the bed of separation, began to dream the sweet dream of a bride in her budding youth. That love of which hitherto she had been unconscious suddenly aroused her with its murmuring music. She wandered a long way up the stream, and saw many a golden mansion and many a grove on either bank; but no foothold could she find now amid the vanished hopes of happiness. She began to say to herself that, when next she met her husband, life should not be insipid nor should the spring come in vain. How very often, in idle disputation or some petty quarrel, had she teased her husband! With all the singleness of a penitent heart she vowed that she would never show impatience again, never oppose her husband's wishes, bear all his commands, and with a tender heart submit to whatever he wished of good or ill; for the husband was all-in-all, the husband was the dearest object of love, the husband was divine.

Sasikala was the only and much-petted daughter of her parents. For this reason, though he had only a small property of his own, Joygopal had no anxieties about the future. His father-in-law

had enough to support them in a village with
royal state.

And then in his old age a son was born untimely to Sasikala's father. To tell the truth,
Sasi was very sore in her mind at this unlooked-
for, improper, and unjust action of her parents;
nor was Joygopal particularly pleased.

The parents' love centred in this son of their
advanced years, and when the newly arrived,
diminutive, sleepy brother-in-law seized with his
two weak tiny fists all the hopes and expectations
of Joygopal, Joygopal found a place in a tea-garden
in Assam.

His friends urged him to look for employment
hard-by, but whether out of a general feeling of
resentment, or knowing the chances of rapid rise in
a tea-garden, Joygopal would not pay heed to anybody. He sent his wife and children to his father-
in-law's, and left for Assam. It was the first separation between husband and wife in their married life.

This incident made Sasikala very angry with
her baby brother. The soreness which may not
pass the lips is felt the more keenly within.
When the little fellow sucked and slept at his
ease, his big sister found a hundred reasons, such
as the rice is cold, the boys are too late for school,

to worry herself and others, day and night, with her petulant humours.

But in a short time the child's mother died. Before her death, she committed her infant son to her daughter's care.

Then did the motherless child easily conquer his sister's heart. With loud whoops he would fling himself upon her, and with right good-will try to get her mouth, nose, eyes within his own tiny mouth; he would seize her hair within his little fists and refuse to give it up ; awaking before the dawn, he would roll over to her side and thrill her with his soft touch, and babble like a noisy brook ; later on, he would call her *jiji* and *jijima*, and in hours of work and rest, by doing forbidden things, eating forbidden food, going to forbidden places, would set up a regular tyranny over her ; then Sasi could resist no longer. She surrendered herself completely to this wayward little tyrant. Since the child had no mother, his influence over her became the greater.

II

The child was named Nilmani. When he was two years old his father fell seriously ill. A letter reached Joygopal asking him to come as quickly as possible. When after much trouble he got leave and arrived, Kaliprasanna's last hour had come.

Before he died Kaliprasanna entrusted Joygopal with the charge of his son, and left a quarter of his estate to his daughter.

So Joygopal gave up his appointment, and came home to look after his property.

After a long time husband and wife met again. When a material body breaks it may be put together again. But when two human beings are divided, after a long separation, they never re-unite at the same place, and to the same time ; for the mind is a living thing, and moment by moment it grows and changes.

In Sasi reunion stirred a new emotion. The numbness of age-long habit in their old marriage was entirely removed by the longing born of separation, and she seemed to win her husband much more closely than before. Had she not vowed in her mind that whatever days might come, and how long soever they might be, she would never let the brightness of this glowing love for her husband be dimmed.

Of this reunion, however, Joygopal felt differently. When they were constantly together before he had been bound to his wife by his interests and idiosyncrasies. His wife was then a living truth in his life, and there would have been a great rent in the web of his daily habit if she were left out. Consequently Joygopal found himself in deep waters at first when he went abroad. But in time this breach in habit was patched up by a new habit.

And this was not all. Formerly his days went by in the most indolent and careless fashion. For the last two years, the stimulus of bettering his condition had stirred so powerfully in his breast that he had nothing else in his thoughts. As compared with the intensity of this new passion, his old life seemed like an unsubstantial shadow. The greatest changes in a woman's nature are wrought by love ; in a man's, by ambition.

Joygopal, when he returned after two years, found his wife not quite the same as of old. To her life his infant brother-in-law had added a new breadth. This part of her life was wholly unfamiliar to him—here he had no communion with his wife. His wife tried hard to share her love for the child with him, but it cannot be said that she succeeded. Sasi would come with the child in her arms, and hold him before her husband with a smiling face

K

—Nilmani would clasp Sasi's neck, and hide his face on her shoulder, and admit no obligation of kindred. Sasi wished that her little brother might show Joygopal all the arts he had learnt to capture a man's mind. But Joygopal was not very keen about it. How could the child show any enthusiasm? Joygopal could not at all understand what there was in the heavy-pated, grave-faced, dusky child that so much love should be wasted on him.

Women quickly understand the ways of love. Sasi at once understood that Joygopal did not care for Nilmani. Henceforth she used to screen her brother with the greatest care—to keep him away from the unloving, repelling look of her husband. Thus the child came to be the treasure of her secret care, the object of her isolated love.

Joygopal was greatly annoyed when Nilmani cried; so Sasi would quickly press the child to her breast, and with her whole heart and soul try to soothe him. And when Nilmani's cry happened to disturb Joygopal's sleep at night, and Joygopal with an expression of displeasure, and in a tortured spirit, growled at the child, Sasi felt humbled and fluttered like a guilty thing. Then would take up the child in her lap, retire to a distance, and in a voice of pleading love, with such endearments as 'my gold, my treasure, my jewel,' lull him to sleep.

Children will fall out for a hundred things. Formerly in such cases, Sasi would punish her children, and side with her brother, for he was motherless. Now the law changed with the judge. Nilmani had often to bear heavy punishment without fault and without inquiry. This wrong went like a dagger to Sasi's heart ; so she would take her punished brother into her room, and with sweets and toys, and by caressing and kissing him, solace as much as she could his stricken heart.

Thus the more Sasi loved Nilmani, the more Joygopal was annoyed with him. On the other hand, the more Joygopal showed his contempt for Nilmani, the more would Sasi bathe the child with the nectar of her love.

And when the fellow Joygopal behaved harshly to his wife, Sasi would minister to him silently, meekly, and with loving-kindness. But inwardly they hurt each other, moment by moment, about Nilmani.

The hidden clash of a silent conflict like this is far harder to bear than an open quarrel.

III

Nilmani's head was the largest part of him. It seemed as if the Creator had blown through a slender stick a big bubble at its top. The doctors feared sometimes that the child might be as frail and as quickly evanescent as a bubble. For a long time he could neither speak nor walk. Looking at his sad grave face, you might think that his parents had unburdened all the sad weight of their advanced years upon the head of this little child.

With his sister's care and nursing, Nilmani passed the period of danger, and arrived at his sixth year.

In the month of Kartik, on the *bhaiphoto*[1] day, Sasi had dressed Nilmani up as a little Babu, in coat and *chadar* and red-bordered *dhoti*, and was giving him the 'brother's mark,' when her outspoken neighbour Tara came in and, for one reason or another, began a quarrel.

' 'Tis no use,' cried she, 'giving the " brother's

---

[1] Lit. the 'brother's mark.' A beautiful and touching ceremony in which a Hindu sister makes a mark of sandalwood paste on the forehead of her brother and utters a formula, 'putting the barrier in Yama's doorway' (figurative for wishing long life). On these occasions, the sisters entertain their brothers and make them presents of clothes, etc.

mark" with so much show and ruining the brother in secret.'

At this Sasi was thunderstruck with astonishment, rage, and pain. Tara repeated the rumour that Sasi and her husband had conspired together to put the minor Nilmani's property up for sale for arrears of rent, and to purchase it in the name of her husband's cousin. When Sasi heard this, she uttered a curse that those who could spread such a foul lie might be stricken with leprosy in the mouth. And then she went weeping to her husband, and told him of the gossip. Joygopal said : 'Nobody can be trusted in these days. Upen is my aunt's son, and I felt quite safe in leaving him in charge of the property. He could not have allowed the *taluk* Hasilpur to fall into arrears and purchase it himself in secret, if I had had the least inkling about it.'

'Won't you sue then ?' asked Sasi in astonishment.

'Sue one's cousin !' said Joygopal. 'Besides, it would be useless, a simple waste of money.'

It was Sasi's supreme duty to trust her husband's word, but Sasi could not. At last her happy home, the domesticity of her love seemed hateful to her. That home life which had once seemed her supreme refuge was nothing more than a cruel snare of self-interest, which had surrounded them, brother and sister, on all sides. She was a woman, single-handed, and she knew not how she could save the helpless Nilmani. The more she thought, the more her heart filled with terror, loathing, and an infinite love for her imperilled little brother. She thought that, if she only knew how, she would appear before the *Lat Saheb*,[1] nay, write to the Maharani herself, to save her brother's property. The Maharani would surely not allow Nilmani's *taluk*[2] of Hasilpur, with an income of seven hundred and fifty-eight rupees a year, to be sold.

When Sasi was thus thinking of bringing her husband's cousin to book by appealing to the Maharani herself, Nilmani was suddenly seized with fever and convulsions.

Joygopal called in the village doctor. When Sasi asked for a better doctor, Joygopal said: 'Why, Matilal isn't a bad sort.'

Sasi fell at his feet, and charged him with an oath on her own head; whereupon Joygopal said: 'Well, I shall send for the doctor from town.'

Sasi lay with Nilmani in her lap, nor would

---

[1] The Viceroy.   [2] Land.

Nilmani let her out of his sight for a minute ; he clung to her lest by some pretence she should escape ; even while he slept he would not loosen his hold of her dress.

Thus the whole day passed, and Joygopal came after nightfall to say that the doctor was not at home ; he had gone to see a patient at a distance. He added that he himself had to leave that very day on account of a lawsuit, and that he had told Matilal, who would regularly call to see the patient.

At night Nilmani wandered in his sleep. As soon as the morning dawned, Sasi, without the least scruple, took a boat with her sick brother, and went straight to the doctor's house. The doctor was at home—he had not left the town. He quickly found lodgings for her, and having installed her under the care of an elderly widow, undertook the treatment of the boy.

The next day Joygopal arrived. Blazing with fury, he ordered his wife to return home with him at once.

' Even if you cut me to pieces, I won't return,' replied his wife.   'You all want to kill my Nilmani, who has no father, no mother, none other than me, but I will save him.'

'Then you remain here, and don't come back to my house,' cried Joygopal indignantly.

Sasi at length fired up. ' *Your* house ! Why, 'tis my brother's ! '

'All right, we'll see,' said Joygopal. The neighbours made a great stir over this incident. 'If you want to quarrel with your husband,' said Tara, ' do so at home. What is the good of leaving your house ? After all, Joygopal is your husband.'

By spending all the money she had with her, and selling her ornaments, Sasi saved her brother from the jaws of death. Then she heard that the big property which they had in Dwarigram, where their dwelling-house stood, the income of which was more than Rs. 1500 a year, had been transferred by Joygopal into his own name with the help of the Jemindar. And now the whole property belonged to them, not to her brother.

When he had recovered from his illness, Nilmani would cry plaintively : ' Let us go home, sister.' His heart was pining for his nephews and nieces, his companions. So he repeatedly said : ' Let us go home, sister, to that old house of ours.' At this Sasi wept. Where was their home ?

But it was no good crying. Her brother had no one else besides herself in the world. Sasi

thought of this, wiped her tears, and, entering the
Zenana of the Deputy Magistrate, Tarini Babu,
appealed to his wife. The Deputy Magistrate
knew Joygopal. That a woman should forsake
her home, and engage in a dispute with her husband
regarding matters of property, greatly incensed
him against Sasi. However, Tarini Babu kept
Sasi diverted, and instantly wrote to Joygopal.
Joygopal put his wife and brother-in-law into a
boat by force, and brought them home.

Husband and wife, after a second separation,
met again for the second time! The decree of
Prajapati![1]

Having got back his old companions after a
long absence, Nilmani was perfectly happy. Seeing
his unsuspecting joy, Sasi felt as if her heart would
break.

IV

The Magistrate was touring in the Mofussil during the cold weather and pitched his tent within
the village to shoot. The Saheb met Nilmani
on the village *maidan*. The other boys gave him
a wide berth, varying Chanakya's couplet a little,
and adding the Saheb to the list of 'the clawed,
the toothed, and the horned beasts.' But grave-

[1] The Hindu god of marriage.

natured Nilmani in imperturbable curiosity serenely gazed at the Saheb.

The Saheb was amused and came up and asked in Bengali : ' You read at the *pathsala* ? '

The boy silently nodded. ' What *pustaks* [1] do you read ? ' asked the Saheb.

As Nilmani did not understand the word *pustak*, he silently fixed his gaze on the Magistrate's face. Nilmani told his sister the story of his meeting the Magistrate with great enthusiasm.

At noon, Joygopal, dressed in trousers, *chapkan*,[2] and *pagri*,[3] went to pay his salams to the Saheb. A crowd of suitors, *chaprasies*,[4] and constables stood about him. Fearing the heat, the Saheb had seated himself at a court-table outside the tent, in the open shade, and placing Joygopal in a chair, questioned him about the state of the village. Having taken the seat of honour in open view of the community, Joygopal swelled inwardly, and thought it would be a good thing if any of the Chakrabartis or Nandis came and saw him there.

At this moment, a woman, closely veiled, and accompanied by Nilmani, came straight up to the Magistrate. She said : ' Saheb, into your hands I

---

[1] A literary word for books. The colloquial will be *boi*.
[2] A *chapkan* is a long coat.   [3] Turban.   [4] Servants.

resign my helpless brother. Save him.' The
Saheb, seeing the large-headed, solemn boy, whose
acquaintance he had already made, and thinking
that the woman must be of a respectable family,
at once stood up and said : ' Please enter the tent.'

The woman said : ' What I have to say I will
say here.'

Joygopal writhed and turned pale. The curious
villagers thought it capital fun, and pressed closer.
But the moment the Saheb lifted his cane they
scampered off.

Holding her brother by the hand, Sasi narrated
the history of the orphan from the beginning.   As
Joygopal tried to interrupt now and then, the
Magistrate thundered with a flushed face, ' *Chup
rao*,' and with the tip of his cane motioned to
Joygopal to leave the chair and stand up.

Joygopal, inwardly raging against Sasi, stood
speechless.   Nilmani nestled up close to his sister,
and listened awe-struck.

When Sasi had finished her story, the Magistrate
put a few questions to Joygopal, and on hearing
his answers, kept silence for a long while, and then
addressed Sasi thus : ' My good woman, though
this matter may not come up before me, still rest
assured I will do all that is needful about it.   You

can return home with your brother without the least misgiving.'

Sasi said: 'Saheb, so long as he does not get back his own home, I dare not take him there. Unless you keep Nilmani with you, none else will be able to save him.'

'And what would you do?' queried the Saheb.

'I will retire to my husband's house,' said Sasi; 'there is nothing to fear for me.'

The Saheb smiled a little, and, as there was nothing else to do, agreed to take charge of this lean, dusty, grave, sedate, gentle Bengali boy whose neck was ringed with amulets.

When Sasi was about to take her leave, the boy clutched her dress. 'Don't be frightened, *baba*, —come,' said the Saheb. With tears streaming behind her veil, Sasi said: 'Do go, my brother, my darling brother—you will meet your sister again!'

Saying this she embraced him and stroked his head and back, and releasing her dress, hastily withdrew; and just then the Saheb put his left arm round him. The child wailed out: 'Sister, oh, my sister!' Sasi turned round at once, and with outstretched arm made a sign of speechless solace, and with a bursting heart withdrew.

Again in that old, ever-familiar house husband and wife met. The decree of Prajapati!

But this union did not last long. For soon after the villagers learnt one morning that Sasi had died of cholera in the night, and had been instantly cremated.

None uttered a word about it. Only neighbour Tara would sometimes be on the point of bursting out, but people would shut up her mouth, saying, 'Hush!'

At parting, Sasi gave her word to her brother they would meet again. Where that word was kept none can tell.

SUBHA

SUBHA

WHEN the girl was given the name of Subhashini,[1] who could have guessed that she would prove dumb? Her two elder sisters were Sukeshini [2] and Suhasini,[3] and for the sake of uniformity her father named his youngest girl Subhashini. She was called Subha for short.

Her two elder sisters had been married with the usual cost and difficulty, and now the youngest daughter lay like a silent weight upon the heart of her parents. All the world seemed to think that, because she did not speak, therefore she did not feel; it discussed her future and its own anxiety freely in her presence. She had understood from her earliest childhood that God had sent her like a curse to her father's house, so she withdrew herself from ordinary people, and tried to live apart. If only they would all forget her she felt she could endure it. But

[1] Sweetly speaking.   [2] Lovely-locked.
[3] Sweetly smiling.

who can forget pain ? Night and day her parents'
minds were aching on her account. Especially
her mother looked upon her as a deformity in
herself. To a mother a daughter is a more closely
intimate part of herself than a son can be ; and a
fault in her is a source of personal shame. Banikantha, Subha's father, loved her rather better
than his other daughters ; her mother regarded
her with aversion as a stain upon her own body.

If Subha lacked speech, she did not lack a pair
of large dark eyes, shaded with long lashes ; and
her lips trembled like a leaf in response to any
thought that rose in her mind.

When we express our thought in words, the
medium is not found easily. There must be a
process of translation, which is often inexact, and
then we fall into error. But black eyes need no
translating ; the mind itself throws a shadow upon
them. In them thought opens or shuts, shines
forth, or goes out in darkness, hangs steadfast like
the setting moon, or, like the swift and restless
lightning, illumines all quarters of the sky. They
who from birth have had no other speech than
the trembling of their lips learn a language of the
eyes, endless in expression, deep as the sea, clear as
the heavens, wherein play dawn and sunset, light

and shadow. The dumb have a lonely grandeur like Nature's own. Wherefore the other children almost dreaded Subha, and never played with her. She was silent and companionless as noontide.

The hamlet where she lived was Chandipur. Its river, small for a river of Bengal, kept to its narrow bounds like a daughter of the middle class. This busy streak of water never overflowed its banks, but went about its duties as though it were a member of every family in the villages beside it. On either side were houses and banks shaded with trees. So stepping from her queenly throne, the river-goddess became a garden deity of each home ; and forgetful of herself, performed her task of endless benediction with swift and cheerful foot.

Banikantha's house looked upon the stream. Every hut and stack in the place could be seen by the passing boatmen. I know not if amid these signs of worldly wealth any one noticed the little girl who, when her work was done, stole away to the waterside, and sat there. But here Nature fulfilled her want of speech, and spoke for her. The murmur of the brook, the voice of the village folk, the songs of the boatmen, the crying of the birds and rustle of trees mingled, and were one with the trembling of her heart. They became

one vast wave of sound, which beat upon her restless soul.　This murmur and movement of Nature
were the dumb girl's language ; that speech of
the dark eyes, which the long lashes shaded, was
the language of the world about her.　From the
trees, where the cicalas chirped, to the quiet stars
there was nothing but signs and gestures, weeping
and sighing.　And in the deep mid-noon, when
the boatmen and fisherfolk had gone to their
dinner, when the villagers slept, and birds were
still, when the ferry-boats were idle, when the great
busy world paused in its toil, and became suddenly
a lonely, awful giant, then beneath the vast im-
pressive heavens there were only dumb Nature
and a dumb girl, sitting very silent—one under
the spreading sunlight, the other where a small
tree cast its shadow.

But Subha was not altogether without friends.
In the stall were two cows, Sarbbashi and Panguli.
They had never heard their names from her lips,
but they knew her footfall.　Though she had no
words, she murmured lovingly and they understood her gentle murmuring better than all speech.
When she fondled them or scolded or coaxed them,
they understood her better than men could do.
Subha would come to the shed, and throw her

arms round Sarbbashi's neck; she would rub her
cheek against her friend's, and Panguli would turn
her great kind eyes and lick her face. The girl
paid them three regular visits every day, and
others that were irregular. Whenever she heard
any words that hurt her, she would come to these
dumb friends out of due time. It was as though
they guessed her anguish of spirit from her quiet
look of sadness. Coming close to her, they
would rub their horns softly against her arms,
and in dumb, puzzled fashion try to comfort
her. Besides these two, there were goats and a
kitten; but Subha had not the same equality of
friendship with them, though they showed the
same attachment. Every time it got a chance,
night or day, the kitten would jump into her lap,
and settle down to slumber, and show its apprecia-
tion of an aid to sleep as Subha drew her soft
fingers over its neck and back.

Subha had a comrade also among the higher
animals, and it is hard to say what were the girl's
relations with him, for he could speak, and his
gift of speech left them without any common
language. He was the youngest boy of the
Gosains, Pratap by name, an idle fellow. After
long effort, his parents had abandoned the hope

that he would ever make his living. Now losels have this advantage, that, though their own folk disapprove of them, they are generally popular with every one else. Having no work to chain them, they become public property. Just as every town needs an open space where all may breathe, so a village needs two or three gentlemen of leisure, who can give time to all; so that, if we are lazy and want a companion, one is to hand.

Pratap's chief ambition was to catch fish. He managed to waste a lot of time this way, and might be seen almost any afternoon so employed. It was thus most often that he met Subha. Whatever he was about, he liked a companion; and, when one is catching fish, a silent companion is best of all. Pratap respected Subha for her taciturnity, and, as every one called her Subha, he showed his affection by calling her Su. Subha used to sit beneath a tamarind, and Pratap, a little distance off, would cast his line. Pratap took with him a small allowance of betel, and Subha prepared it for him. And I think that, sitting and gazing a long while, she desired ardently to bring some great help to Pratap, to be of real aid, to prove by any means that she was not a useless burden to the world. But there was nothing to do. Then she turned to the Creator in prayer for some rare power, that by an astonishing miracle she might startle Pratap into exclaiming : " My ! I never dreamt our Su could have done this ! "

Only think ! if Subha had been a water nymph, she might have risen slowly from the river, bringing the gem of a snake's crown to the landing-place. Then Pratap, leaving his paltry fishing, might dive into the lower world, and see there, on a golden bed in a palace of silver, whom else but dumb little Su, Banikantha's child? Yes, our Su, the only daughter of the king of that shining city of jewels ! But that might not be, it was impossible. Not that anything is really impossible, but Su had been born, not into the royal house of Patalpur,[1] but into Banikantha's family, and she knew no means of astonishing the Gosains' boy.

Gradually she grew up. Gradually she began to find herself. A new inexpressible consciousness like a tide from the central places of the sea, when the moon is full, swept through her. She saw herself, questioned herself, but no answer came that she could understand.

Once upon a time, late on a night of full moon,

[1] The Lower World.

she slowly opened her door, and peeped out timidly. Nature, herself at full moon, like lonely Subha, was looking down on the sleeping earth. Her strong young life beat within her; joy and sadness filled her being to its brim; she reached the limits even of her own illimitable loneliness, nay, passed beyond them. Her heart was heavy, and she could not speak! At the skirts of this silent, troubled Mother there stood a silent troubled girl.

The thought of her marriage filled her parents with an anxious care. People blamed them, and even talked of making them outcasts. Banikantha was well off; they had fish-curry twice daily; and consequently he did not lack enemies. Then the women interfered, and Bani went away for a few days. Presently he returned, and said: "We must go to Calcutta."

They got ready to go to this strange country. Subha's heart was heavy with tears, like a mist-wrapt dawn. With a vague fear that had been gathering for days, she dogged her father and mother like a dumb animal. With her large eyes wide open, she scanned their faces as though she wished to learn something. But not a word did they vouchsafe. One afternoon in the midst of

all this, as Pratap was fishing, he laughed : 'So then,
Su, they have caught your bridegroom, and you
are going to be married !   Mind you don't forget
me altogether !'   Then he turned his mind again
to his fish.   As a stricken doe looks in the hunter's
face, asking in silent agony: 'What have I done
to you ?' so Subha looked at Pratap.   That day
she sat no longer beneath her tree.   Banikantha,
having finished his nap, was smoking in his bedroom when Subha dropped down at his feet and
burst out weeping as she gazed towards him.
Banikantha tried to comfort her, and his cheek
grew wet with tears.

It was settled that on the morrow they should
go to Calcutta.   Subha went to the cow-shed to
bid farewell to her childhood's comrades.   She fed
them with her hand ; she clasped their necks ; she
looked into their faces, and tears fell fast from
the eyes which spoke for her.   That night was
the tenth of the moon.   Subha left her room, and
flung herself down on her grassy couch beside her
dear river.   It was as if she threw her arms about
Earth, her strong, silent mother, and tried to say :
'Do not let me leave you, mother.   Put your
arms about me, as I have put mine about you, and
hold me fast.'

One day in a house in Calcutta, Subha's mother dressed her up with great care. She imprisoned her hair, knotting it up in laces, she hung her about with ornaments, and did her best to kill her natural beauty. Subha's eyes filled with tears. Her mother, fearing they would grow swollen with weeping, scolded her harshly, but the tears disregarded the scolding. The bridegroom came with a friend to inspect the bride. Her parents were dizzy with anxiety and fear when they saw the god arrive to select the beast for his sacrifice. Behind the stage, the mother called her instructions aloud, and increased her daughter's weeping twofold, before she sent her into the examiner's presence. The great man, after scanning her a long time, observed : ' Not so bad.'

He took special note of her tears, and thought she must have a tender heart. He put it to her credit in the account, arguing that the heart, which to-day was distressed at leaving her parents, would presently prove a useful possession. Like the oyster's pearls, the child's tears only increased her value, and he made no other comment.

The almanac was consulted, and the marriage took place on an auspicious day. Having delivered over their dumb girl into another's hands, Subha's parents returned home. Thank God! Their caste in this and their safety in the next world were assured! The bridegroom's work lay in the west, and shortly after the marriage he took his wife thither.

In less than ten days every one knew that the bride was dumb! At least, if any one did not, it was not her fault, for she deceived no one. Her eyes told them everything, though no one understood her. She looked on every hand; she found no speech; she missed the faces, familiar from birth, of those who had understood a dumb girl's language. In her silent heart there sounded an endless, voiceless weeping, which only the Searcher of Hearts could hear.

Using both eyes and ears *this* time, her lord made another careful examination, using his ears this time as well as his eyes, and married a second wife who could speak.

THE POSTMASTER

THE POSTMASTER

THE postmaster first took up his duties in the village of Ulapur. Though the village was a small one, there was an indigo factory near by, and the proprietor, an Englishman, had managed to get a post office established.

Our postmaster belonged to Calcutta. He felt like a fish out of water in this remote village. His office and living-room were in a dark thatched shed, not far from a green, slimy pond, surrounded on all sides by a dense growth.

The men employed in the indigo factory had no leisure ; moreover, they were hardly desirable companions for decent folk. Nor is a Calcutta boy an adept in the art of associating with others. Among strangers he appears either proud or ill at ease. At any rate, the postmaster had but little company ; nor had he much to do.

At times he tried his hand at writing a verse or two. That the movement of the leaves and the

clouds of the sky were enough to fill life with joy
—such were the sentiments to which he sought
to give expression.   But God knows that the
poor fellow would have felt it as the gift of a
new life, if some genie of the *Arabian Nights*
had in one night swept away the trees, leaves
and all, and replaced them with a macadamised
road, hiding the clouds from view with rows of
tall houses.

The postmaster's salary was small.   He had to
cook his own meals, which he used to share with
Ratan, an orphan girl of the village, who did odd
jobs for him.

When in the evening the smoke began to curl
up from the village cow-sheds,[1] and the cicalas
chirped in every bush ; when the faquirs of the
Baül sect sang their shrill songs in their daily
meeting-place, when any poet, who had attempted
to watch the movement of the leaves in the dense
bamboo thickets, would have felt a ghostly shiver
run down his back, the postmaster would light his
little lamp, and call out ' Ratan.'

Ratan would sit outside waiting for this call,
and, instead of coming in at once, would reply :
' Did you call me, sir ? '

---

[1] Smoky fires are lit in the cow-sheds to drive off mosquitoes.

' What are you doing ? ' the postmaster would ask.

' I must be going to light the kitchen fire,' would be the answer.

And the postmaster would say : ' Oh, let the kitchen fire be for awhile ; light me my pipe first.'

At last Ratan would enter, with puffed-out cheeks, vigorously blowing into a flame a live coal to light the tobacco. This would give the post-master an opportunity of conversing. ' Well, Ratan,' perhaps he would begin, ' do you remember anything of your mother ? ' That was a fertile subject. Ratan partly remembered, and partly didn't. Her father had been fonder of her than her mother ; him she recollected more vividly. He used to come home in the evening after his work, and one or two evenings stood out more clearly than others, like pictures in her memory. Ratan would squat on the floor near the postmaster's feet, as memories crowded in upon her. She called to mind a little brother that she had—and how on some bygone cloudy day she had played at fishing with him on the edge of the pond, with a twig for a make-believe fishing-rod. Such little incidents would drive out greater events from her mind. Thus, as they talked, it

M

would often get very late, and the postmaster
would feel too lazy to do any cooking at all.
Ratan would then hastily light the fire, and toast
some unleavened bread, which, with the cold
remnants of the morning meal, was enough for
their supper.

On some evenings, seated at his desk in the
corner of the big empty shed, the postmaster too
would call up memories of his own home, of his
mother and his sister, of those for whom in his
exile his heart was sad,—memories which were
always haunting him, but which he could not
talk about with the men of the factory, though he
found himself naturally recalling them aloud in the
presence of the simple little girl. And so it came
about that the girl would allude to his people as
mother, brother, and sister,[1] as if she had known
them all her life. In fact, she had a complete
picture of each one of them painted in her little
heart.

One noon, during a break in the rains, there
was a cool soft breeze blowing ; the smell of the
damp grass and leaves in the hot sun felt like the
warm breathing of the tired earth on one's body.

[1] Family servants call the master and mistress father and mother and
the children elder brothers and sisters.

A persistent bird went on all the afternoon repeating the burden of its one complaint in Nature's audience chamber.

The postmaster had nothing to do. The shimmer of the freshly washed leaves, and the banked-up remnants of the retreating rain-clouds were sights to see; and the postmaster was watching them, and thinking to himself: 'Oh, if only some kindred soul were near—just one loving human being whom I could hold near my heart!' This was exactly, he went on to think, what that bird was trying to say, and it was the same feeling which the murmuring leaves were striving to express. But no one knows, or would believe, that such an idea might also take possession of an ill-paid village postmaster in the deep, silent midday interval of his work.

The postmaster sighed, and called out 'Ratan.' Ratan was then sprawling beneath the guava-tree, busily engaged in eating unripe guavas. At the voice of her master, she ran up breathlessly, saying: 'Were you calling me, Dada?'[1] 'I was thinking,' said the postmaster, 'of teaching you to read,' and then for the rest of the afternoon he taught her the alphabet.

[1] Dada = elder brother.

Thus, in a very short time, Ratan had got as far as the double consonants.

It seemed as though the showers of the season would never end. Canals, ditches, and hollows were all overflowing with water. Day and night the patter of rain was heard, and the croaking of frogs. The village roads became impassable, and marketing had to be done in punts.

One heavily clouded morning, the postmaster's little pupil had been long waiting outside the door for her call, but, not hearing it as usual, she took up her dog-eared book, and slowly entered the room. She found her master stretched out on his pallet, and, thinking he was resting, she was about to retire on tip-toe, when she suddenly heard her name—' Ratan ! ' She turned at once and asked : ' Were you sleeping, Dada ? ' The postmaster in a plaintive voice said : ' I am not well. Feel my head ; is it very hot ? '

In the loneliness of his exile, and in the gloom of the rains, his ailing body needed a little tender nursing. He longed to remember the touch on the forehead of soft hands with tinkling bracelets, to imagine the presence of loving womanhood, the nearness of mother and sister. And the exile was not disappointed. Ratan ceased to be a little girl.

She at once stepped into the post of mother, called in the village doctor, gave the patient his pills at the proper intervals, sat up all night by his pillow, cooked his gruel for him, and every now and then asked : ' Are you feeling a little better, Dada ? '

It was some time before the postmaster, with weakened body, was able to leave his sick-bed. ' No more of this,' said he with decision. ' I must get a transfer.' He at once wrote off to Calcutta an application for a transfer, on the ground of the unhealthiness of the place.

Relieved from her duties as nurse, Ratan again took up her old place outside the door. But she no longer heard the same old call. She would sometimes peep inside furtively to find the post-master sitting on his chair, or stretched on his pallet, and staring absent-mindedly into the air. While Ratan was awaiting her call, the postmaster was awaiting a reply to his application. The girl read her old lessons over and over again—her great fear was lest, when the call came, she might be found wanting in the double consonants. At last, after a week, the call did come one evening. With an overflowing heart Ratan rushed into the room with her — ' Were you calling me, Dada ? '

The postmaster said : ' I am going away to-morrow, Ratan.'

' Where are you going, Dada ? '

' I am going home.'

' When will you come back ? '

' I am not coming back.

Ratan asked no other question. The post-master, of his own accord, went on to tell her that his application for a transfer had been rejected, so he had resigned his post, and was going home.

For a long time neither of them spoke another word. The lamp went on dimly burning, and from a leak in one corner of the thatch water dripped steadily into an earthen vessel on the floor beneath it.

After a while Ratan rose, and went off to the kitchen to prepare the meal ; but she was not so quick about it as on other days. Many new things to think of had entered her little brain. When the postmaster had finished his supper, the girl suddenly asked him : ' Dada, will you take me to your home ? '

The postmaster laughed. ' What an idea ! ' said he ; but he did not think it necessary to explain to the girl wherein lay the absurdity.

That whole night, in her waking and in her

dreams, the postmaster's laughing reply haunted her—'What an idea !'

On getting up in the morning, the postmaster found his bath ready. He had stuck to his Calcutta habit of bathing in water drawn and kept in pitchers, instead of taking a plunge in the river as was the custom of the village. For some reason or other, the girl could not ask him about the time of his departure, so she had fetched the water from the river long before sunrise, that it should be ready as early as he might want it. After the bath came a call for Ratan. She entered noiselessly, and looked silently into her master's face for orders. The master said : 'You need not be anxious about my going away, Ratan ; I shall tell my successor to look after you.' These words were kindly meant, no doubt : but inscrutable are the ways of a woman's heart !

Ratan had borne many a scolding from her master without complaint, but these kind words she could not bear. She burst out weeping, and said : 'No, no, you need not tell anybody anything at all about me ; I don't want to stay on here.'

The postmaster was dumbfounded. He had never seen Ratan like this before.

The new incumbent duly arrived, and the postmaster, having given over charge, prepared to depart. Just before starting he called Ratan, and said : 'Here is something for you ; I hope it will keep you for some little time.' He brought out from his pocket the whole of his month's salary, retaining only a trifle for his travelling expenses. Then Ratan fell at his feet and cried : 'Oh, Dada, I pray you, don't give me anything, don't in any way trouble about me,' and then she ran away out of sight.

The postmaster heaved a sigh, took up his carpet bag, put his umbrella over his shoulder, and, accompanied by a man carrying his many-coloured tin trunk, he slowly made for the boat.

When he got in and the boat was under way, and the rain-swollen river, like a stream of tears welling up from the earth, swirled and sobbed at her bows, then he felt a sort of pain at heart ; the grief-stricken face of a village girl seemed to represent for him the great unspoken pervading grief of Mother Earth herself. At one time he had an impulse to go back, and bring away along with him that lonesome waif, forsaken of the world. But the wind had just filled the sails, the boat had got well into the middle of the turbulent current, and already the village was left behind, and its outlying burning-ground came in sight.

So the traveller, borne on the breast of the swift-flowing river, consoled himself with philosophical reflections on the numberless meetings and partings going on in the world—on death, the great parting, from which none returns.

But Ratan had no philosophy. She was wandering about the post office in a flood of tears. It may be that she had still a lurking hope in some corner of her heart that her Dada would return, and that is why she could not tear herself away. Alas for the foolish human heart!

THE RIVER STAIRS

THE RIVER STAIRS

If you wish to hear of days gone by, sit on this step of mine, and lend your ears to the murmur of the rippling water.

The month of *Ashwin* (September) was about to begin. The river was in full flood. Only four of my steps peeped above the surface. The water had crept up to the low-lying parts of the bank, where the *kachu* plant grew dense beneath the branches of the mango grove. At that bend of the river, three old brick-heaps towered above the water around them. The fishing-boats, moored to the trunks of the *babla* trees on the bank, rocked on the heaving flow-tide at dawn. The path of tall grasses on the sandbank had caught the newly risen sun ; they had just begun to flower, and were not yet in full bloom.

The little boats puffed out their tiny sails on the sunlit river. The Brahmin priest had come to bathe with his ritual vessels. The women

173

arrived in twos and threes to draw water. I knew this was the time of Kusum's coming to the bathing-stairs.

But that morning I missed her. Bhuban and Swarno mourned at the *ghat*.[1] They said that their friend had been led away to her husband's house, which was a place far away from the river, with strange people, strange houses, and strange roads.

In time she almost faded out of my mind. A year passed. The women at the *ghat* now rarely talked of Kusum. But one evening I was startled by the touch of the long familiar feet. Ah, yes, but those feet were now without anklets, they had lost their old music.

Kusum had become a widow. They said that her husband had worked in some far-off place, and that she had met him only once or twice. A letter brought her the news of his death. A widow at eight years old, she had rubbed out the wife's red mark from her forehead, stripped off her bangles, and come back to her old home by the Ganges. But she found few of her old play-mates there. Of them, Bhuban, Swarno, and Amala were married, and gone away ; only Sarat

1 Bathing-place.

remained, and she too, they said, would be wed in December next.

As the Ganges rapidly grows to fulness with the coming of the rains, even so did Kusum day by day grow to the fulness of beauty and youth. But her dull-coloured robe, her pensive face, and quiet manners drew a veil over her youth, and hid it from men's eyes as in a mist. Ten years slipped away, and none seemed to have noticed that Kusum had grown up.

One morning such as this, at the end of a far-off September, a tall, young, fair-skinned Sanyasi, coming I know not whence, took shelter in the Shiva temple in front of me. His arrival was noised abroad in the village. The women left their pitchers behind, and crowded into the temple to bow to the holy man.

The crowd increased day by day. The Sanyasi's fame rapidly spread among the womenkind. One day he would recite the *Bhágbat*, another day he would expound the *Gita*, or hold forth upon a holy book in the temple. Some sought him for counsel, some for spells, some for medicines.

So months passed away. In April, at the time of the solar eclipse, vast crowds came here to bathe in the Ganges. A fair was held under the *babla* tree. Many of the pilgrims went to visit the Sanyasi, and among them were a party of women from the village where Kusum had been married.

It was morning. The Sanyasi was counting his beads on my steps, when all of a sudden one of the women pilgrims nudged another, and said : 'Why! He is our Kusum's husband!' Another parted her veil a little in the middle with two fingers and cried out : 'Oh dear me! So it is! He is the younger son of the Chattergu family of our village !' Said a third, who made little parade of her veil : 'Ah! he has got exactly the same brow, nose, and eyes !' Yet another woman, without turning to the Sanyasi, stirred the water with her pitcher, and sighed : 'Alas! That young man is no more ; he will not come back. Bad luck to Kusum !'

But, objected one, 'He had not such a big beard' ; and another, 'He was not so thin' ; or 'He was most probably not so tall.' That settled the question for the time, and the matter spread no further.

One evening, as the full moon arose, Kusum came and sat upon my last step above the water, and cast her shadow upon me.

There was no other at the *ghat* just then. The

crickets were chirping about me. The din of brass gongs and bells had ceased in the temple— the last wave of sound grew fainter and fainter, until it merged like the shade of a sound in the dim groves of the farther bank. On the dark water of the Ganges lay a line of glistening moonlight. On the bank above, in bush and hedge, under the porch of the temple, in the base of ruined houses, by the side of the tank, in the palm grove, gathered shadows of fantastic shape. The bats swung from the *chhatim* boughs. Near the houses the loud clamour of the jackals rose and sank into silence.

Slowly the Sanyasi came out of the temple. Descending a few steps of the *ghāt* he saw a woman sitting alone, and was about to go back, when suddenly Kusum raised her head, and looked behind her. The veil slipped away from her. The moonlight fell upon her face, as she looked up.

The owl flew away hooting over their heads. Starting at the sound, Kusum came to herself and put the veil back on her head. Then she bowed low at the Sanyasi's feet.

He gave her blessing and asked: 'Who are you?'
She replied : 'I am called Kusum.'
No other word was spoken that night. Kusum

N

went slowly back to her house which was hard by. But the Sanyasi remained sitting on my steps for long hours that night. At last when the moon passed from the east to the west, and the Sanyasi's shadow, shifting from behind, fell in front of him, he rose up and entered the temple.

Henceforth I saw Kusum come daily to bow at his feet. When he expounded the holy books, she stood in a corner listening to him. After finishing his morning service, he used to call her to himself and speak on religion. She could not have understood it all ; but, listening attentively in silence, she tried to understand it. As he directed her, so she acted implicitly. She daily served at the temple—ever alert in the god's worship—gathering flowers for the *puja*, and drawing water from the Ganges to wash the temple floor.

The winter was drawing to its close. We had cold winds. But now and then in the evening the warm spring breeze would blow unexpectedly from the south ; the sky would lose its chilly aspect ; pipes would sound, and music be heard in the village after a long silence. The boatmen would set their boats drifting down the current, stop rowing, and begin to sing the songs of Krishna. This was the season.

Just then I began to miss Kusum.   For some time she had given up visiting the temple, the *ghat*, or the Sanyasi.

What happened next I do not know, but after a while the two met together on my steps one evening.

With downcast looks, Kusum asked : ' Master, did you send for me ? '

' Yes, why do I not see you ?   Why have you grown neglectful of late in serving the gods ? '

She kept silent.

' Tell me your thoughts without reserve.'

Half averting her face, she replied : ' I am a sinner, Master, and hence I have failed in the worship.'

The Sanyasi said : ' Kusum, I know there is unrest in your heart.'

She gave a slight start, and, drawing the end of her sári over her face, she sat down on the step at the Sanyasi's feet, and wept.

He moved a little away, and said : ' Tell me what you have in your heart, and I shall show you the way to peace.'

She replied in a tone of unshaken faith, stopping now and then for words : ' If you bid me, I must speak out.   But, then, I cannot explain it clearly.

You, Master, must have guessed it all.   I adored
one as a god, I worshipped him, and the bliss of that
devotion filled my heart to fulness.   But one night
I dreamt that the lord of my heart was sitting in
a garden somewhere, clasping my right hand in
his left, and whispering to me of love.   The
whole scene did not appear to me at all strange.
The dream vanished, but its hold on me remained.
Next day when I beheld him he appeared in
another light than before.   That dream-picture
continued to haunt my mind.   I fled far from
him in fear, and the picture clung to me.   Thence-
forth my heart has known no peace,—all has
grown dark within me !'

While she was wiping her tears and telling
this tale, I felt that the Sanyasi was firmly pressing
my stone surface with his right foot.

Her speech done, the Sanyasi said :

'You must tell me whom you saw in your
dream.'

With folded hands, she entreated : 'I cannot.'

He insisted : 'You must tell me who he was.'

Wringing her hands she asked : 'Must I tell it ?'

He replied : 'Yes, you must.'

Then crying, 'You are he, Master !' she fell
on her face on my stony bosom, and sobbed.

When she came to herself, and sat up, the Sanyasi said slowly : ' I am leaving this place to-night that you may not see me again. Know that I am a Sanyasi, not belonging to this world. *You* must forget me.'

Kusum replied in a low voice : 'It will be so, Master.'

The Sanyasi said : ' I take my leave.'

Without a word more Kusum bowed to him, and placed the dust of his feet on her head. He left the place.

The moon set ; the night grew dark. I heard a splash in the water. The wind raved in the darkness, as if it wanted to blow out all the stars of the sky.

THE CASTAWAY

THE CASTAWAY

Towards evening the storm was at its height. From the terrific downpour of rain, the crash of thunder, and the repeated flashes of lightning, you might think that a battle of the gods and demons was raging in the skies. Black clouds waved like the Flags of Doom. The Ganges was lashed into a fury, and the trees of the gardens on either bank swayed from side to side with sighs and groans.

In a closed room of one of the riverside houses at Chandernagore, a husband and his wife were seated on a bed spread on the floor, intently discussing. An earthen lamp burned beside them.

The husband, Sharat, was saying : ' I wish you would stay on a few days more ; you would then be able to return home quite strong again.'

The wife, Kiran, was saying : ' I have quite recovered already. It will not, cannot possibly, do me any harm to go home now.'

Every married person will at once understand that the conversation was not quite so brief as I have reported it. The matter was not difficult, but the arguments for and against did not advance it towards a solution. Like a rudderless boat, the discussion kept turning round and round the same point ; and at last it threatened to be over- whelmed in a flood of tears.

Sharat said : 'The doctor thinks you should stop here a few days longer.'

Kiran replied: 'Your doctor knows everything !'

'Well,' said Sharat, 'you know that just now all sorts of illness are abroad. You would do well to stop here a month or two more.'

'And at this moment I suppose every one in this place is perfectly well !'

What had happened was this : Kiran was a universal favourite with her family and neighbours, so that, when she fell seriously ill, they were all anxious. The village wiseacres thought it shame- less for her husband to make so much fuss about a mere wife and even to suggest a change of air, and asked if Sharat supposed that no woman had ever been ill before, or whether he had found out that the folk of the place to which he meant to take her were immortal. Did he imagine that the writ of Fate did not run there? But Sharat and his mother turned a deaf ear to them, thinking that the little life of their darling was of greater importance than the united wisdom of a village. People are wont to reason thus when danger threatens their loved ones. So Sharat went to Chandernagore, and Kiran recovered, though she was still very weak. There was a pinched look on her face which filled the beholder with pity, and made his heart tremble, as he thought how narrowly she had escaped death.

Kiran was fond of society and amusement; the loneliness of her riverside villa did not suit her at all. There was nothing to do, there were no interesting neighbours, and she hated to be busy all day with medicine and dieting. There was no fun in measuring doses and making fomentations. Such was the subject discussed in their closed room on this stormy evening.

So long as Kiran deigned to argue, there was a chance of a fair fight. When she ceased to reply, and with a toss of her head disconsolately looked the other way, the poor man was disarmed. He was on the point of surrendering unconditionally when a servant shouted a message through the shut door.

Sharat got up, and, opening the door, learnt that a boat had been upset in the storm, and that one of the occupants, a young Brahmin boy, had succeeded in swimming ashore in their garden.

Kiran was at once her own sweet self, and set to work to get out some dry clothes for the boy. She then warmed a cup of milk, and invited him to her room.

The boy had long curly hair, big expressive eyes, and no sign yet of hair on the face. Kiran, after getting him to drink some milk, asked him all about himself.

He told her that his name was Nilkanta, and that he belonged to a theatrical troupe. They were coming to play in a neighbouring villa when the boat had suddenly foundered in the storm. He had no idea what had become of his companions. He was a good swimmer, and had just managed to reach the shore.

The boy stayed with them. His narrow escape from a terrible death made Kiran take a warm interest in him. Sharat thought the boy's appearance at this moment rather a good thing, as his wife would now have something to amuse her, and might be persuaded to stay on for some time longer. Her mother-in-law, too, was pleased

at the prospect of profiting their Brahmin guest by
her kindness. And Nilkanta himself was delighted
at his double escape from his master and from
the other world, as well as at finding a home in
this wealthy family.

But in a short while Sharat and his mother
changed their opinion, and longed for his departure.
The boy found a secret pleasure in smoking
Sharat's hookas; he would calmly go off in
pouring rain with Sharat's best silk umbrella for a
stroll through the village, and make friends with
all whom he met. Moreover, he had got hold of a
mongrel village dog which he petted so recklessly
that it came indoors with muddy paws, and
left tokens of its visit on Sharat's spotless bed.
Then he gathered about him a devoted band of
boys of all sorts and sizes, and the result was that
not a solitary mango in the neighbourhood had a
chance of ripening that season.

There is no doubt that Kiran had a hand in
spoiling the boy. Sharat often warned her about
it, but she would not listen to him. She made a
dandy of him with Sharat's cast-off clothes, and
gave him new ones too. And because she felt
drawn towards him, and also had a curiosity to
know more about him, she was constantly calling

him to her own room. After her bath and mid-day
meal Kiran would be seated on the bedstead with
her betel-leaf box by her side ; and while her
maid combed and dried her hair, Nilkanta would
stand in front and recite pieces out of his repertory
with appropriate gesture and song, his elf-locks
waving wildly. Thus the long afternoon hours
passed merrily away. Kiran would often try to
persuade Sharat to sit with her as one of the
audience, but Sharat, who had taken a cordial
dislike to the boy, refused, nor could Nilkanta do
his part half so well when Sharat was there. His
mother would sometimes be lured by the hope of
hearing sacred names in the recitation ; but love
of her mid-day sleep speedily overcame devotion,
and she lay lapped in dreams.

The boy often got his ears boxed and pulled
by Sharat, but as this was nothing to what he
had been used to as a member of the troupe,
he did not mind it in the least. In his short ex-
perience of the world he had come to the conclusion
that, as the earth consisted of land and water, so
human life was made up of eatings and beatings,
and that the beatings largely predominated.

It was hard to tell Nilkanta's age. If it was
about fourteen or fifteen, then his face was too old

for his years ; if seventeen or eighteen, then it was too young. He was either a man too early or a boy too late. The fact was that, joining the theatrical band when very young, he had played the parts of Radhika, Damaynti, Sita, and Bidya's Companion. A thoughtful Providence so arranged things that he grew to the exact stature that his manager required, and then growth ceased. Since every one saw how small he was, and he himself felt small, he did not receive due respect for his years. These causes, natural and artificial, combined to make him sometimes seem immature for seventeen years, and at other times a lad of fourteen but far too knowing for seventeen. And as no sign of hair appeared on his face, the confusion became greater. Either because he smoked or because he used language beyond his years, his lips puckered into lines that showed him to be old and hard ; but innocence and youth shone in his large eyes. I fancy that his heart remained young, but the hot glare of publicity had been a forcing-house that ripened untimely his outward aspect.

In the quiet shelter of Sharat's house and garden at Chandernagore, Nature had leisure to work her way unimpeded. He had lingered in a kind of unnatural youth, but now he silently and swiftly

overpassed that stage.   His seventeen or eighteen
years came to adequate revelation. No one observed
the change, and its first sign was this, that when
Kiran treated him like a boy, he felt ashamed.
When the gay Kiran one day proposed that he
should play the part of lady's companion, the idea
of woman's dress hurt him, though he could not
say why.   So now, when she called for him to act
over again his old characters, he disappeared.   It
never occurred to him that he was even now not
much more than a lad-of-all-work in a strolling
company.   He even made up his mind to pick
up a little education from Sharat's factor.   But,
because Nilkanta was the pet of his master's wife,
the factor could not endure the sight of him.   Also,
his restless training made it impossible for him to
keep his mind long engaged ; presently, the alphabet
did a misty dance before his eyes.   He would sit
long enough with an open book on his lap, leaning
against a *champak* bush beside the Ganges.   The
waves sighed below, boats floated past, birds flitted
and twittered restlessly above.   What thoughts
passed through his mind as he looked down on
that book he alone knew, if indeed he did know.
He never advanced from one word to another, but
the glorious thought that he was actually reading

a book filled his soul with exultation. Whenever
a boat went by, he lifted his book, and pretended
to be reading hard, shouting at the top of his voice.
But his energy dropped as soon as the audience
was gone.

Formerly he sang his songs automatically, but
now their tunes stirred in his mind. Their words
were of little import, and full of trifling alliteration.
Even the little meaning they had was beyond his
comprehension ; yet when he sang—

> Twice-born [1] bird ! ah ! wherefore stirred
>   To wrong our royal lady ?
> Goose, ah ! say why wilt thou slay
>   Her in forest shady ? [2]

then he felt as if transported to another world,
and to far other folk. This familiar earth and
his own poor life became music, and he was transformed. That tale of goose and king's daughter
flung upon the mirror of his mind a picture of
surpassing beauty. It is impossible to say what he
imagined he himself was, but the destitute little
slave of the theatrical troupe faded from his
memory.

When with evening the child of want lies down,
dirty and hungry, in his squalid home, and hears

[1] Once in the egg, and again once out of the egg.
[2] See note on Damaynti.

of prince and princess and fabled gold, then in the
dark hovel with its dim flickering candle, his mind
springs free from her bonds of poverty and misery,
and walks in fresh beauty and glowing raiment,
strong beyond all fear of hindrance, through that
fairy realm where all is possible.

Even so, this drudge of wandering players
fashioned himself and his world anew, as he moved
in spirit amid his songs. The lapping water,
rustling leaves, and calling birds; the goddess who
had given shelter to him, the helpless, the God-
forsaken; her gracious, lovely face, her exquisite
arms with their shining bangles, her rosy feet as
soft as flower-petals; all these by some magic
became one with the music of his song. When the
singing ended, the mirage faded, and Nilkanta of
the stage appeared again, with his wild elf-locks.
Fresh from the complaints of his neighbour, the
owner of the despoiled mango-orchard, Sharat
would come and box his ears, and cuff him. The
boy Nilkanta, the misleader of adoring youths,
went forth once more, to make ever new mischief
by land and water and in the branches that are
above the earth.

Shortly after the advent of Nilkanta, Sharat's
younger brother, Satish, came to spend his college

vacation with them.   Kiran was hugely pleased at
finding a fresh occupation.   She and Satish were
of the same age, and the time passed pleasantly in
games and quarrels and makings-up and laughter
and even tears.   Suddenly she would clasp him
over the eyes, from behind, with vermilion-stained
hands, she would write ' monkey ' on his back,
and sometimes bolt the door on him from outside
amidst peals of laughter.   Satish in his turn did
not take things lying down ; he would take her
keys and rings, he would put pepper among her
betel ; he would tie her to the bed when she was
not looking.

Meanwhile, heaven only knows what possessed
poor Nilkanta.   He was suddenly filled with a
bitterness which he must avenge on somebody or
something.   He thrashed his devoted boy-followers
for no fault, and sent them away crying.   He
would kick his pet mongrel till it made the skies
resound with its whinings.   When he went out
for a walk, he would litter his path with twigs
and leaves beaten from the roadside shrubs with
his cane.

Kiran liked to see people enjoying good fare.
Nilkanta had an immense capacity for eating, and
never refused a good thing, however often it was

offered. So Kiran liked to send for him to have his meals in her presence, and ply him with delicacies, happy in the bliss of seeing this Brahmin boy eat to satiety. After Satish's arrival she had much less spare time on her hands, and was seldom present when Nilkanta's meals were served. Before, her absence made no difference to the boy's appetite, and he would not rise till he had drained his cup of milk, and rinsed it thoroughly with water.[1]

But now, if Kiran was not present to ask him to try this and that, he was miserable, and nothing tasted right. He would get up without eating much, and say to the serving-maid in a choking voice : 'I am not hungry.' He thought in imagination that the news of his repeated refusal, 'I am not hungry,' would reach Kiran; he pictured her concern, and hoped that she would send for him, and press him to eat. But nothing of the sort happened. Kiran never knew, and never sent for him ; and the maid finished whatever he left. He would then put out the lamp in his room, and throw himself on his bed in the darkness, burying his head in the pillow in a paroxysm of sobs. What was his grievance ? Against whom ? And

---

[1] A habit which was relic from his days of poverty, when milk was too rare a luxury to allow of even its stains in the cup being wasted.

from whom did he expect redress ? At last, when
none else came, Mother Sleep soothed with her soft
caresses the wounded heart of the motherless lad.

Nilkanta came to the unshakable conviction
that Satish was poisoning Kiran's mind against him.
If Kiran was absent-minded, and had not her usual
smile, he would jump to the conclusion that some
trick of Satish had made her angry with him. He
took to praying to the gods, with all the fervour of
his hate, to make him at the next rebirth Satish,
and Satish him. He had an idea that a Brahmin's
wrath could never be in vain ; and the more he
tried to consume Satish with the fire of his curses,
the more did his own heart burn within him. And
upstairs he would hear Satish laughing and joking
with his sister-in-law.

Nilkanta never dared openly to show his enmity
to Satish. But he would contrive a hundred petty
ways of causing him annoyance. When Satish
went for a swim in the river, and left his soap on
the steps of the bathing-place, on coming back for
it he would find that it had disappeared. Once
he found his favourite striped tunic floating past
him on the water, and thought it had been blown
away by the wind.

One day Kiran, desiring to entertain Satish,

sent for Nilkanta to recite as usual, but he stood there in gloomy silence. Quite surprised, Kiran asked him what was the matter. But he remained silent. And when again pressed by her to repeat some particular favourite piece of hers, he answered : ' I don't remember,' and walked away.

At last the time came for their return home. Everybody was busy packing up. Satish was going with them. But to Nilkanta nobody said a word. The question whether he was to go or not seemed not to have occurred to anybody.

The question, as a matter of fact, had been raised by Kiran, who had proposed to take him along with them. But her husband and his mother and brother had all objected so strenuously that she let the matter drop. A couple of days before they were to start, she sent for the boy, and with kind words advised him to go back to his own home.

So many days had he felt neglected that this touch of kindness was too much for him ; he burst into tears. Kiran's eyes were also brimming over. She was filled with remorse at the thought that she had created a tie of affection, which could not be permanent.

But Satish was much annoyed at the blubbering

of this overgrown boy. 'Why does the fool stand there howling instead of speaking?' said he. When Kiran scolded him for an unfeeling creature, he replied : 'Sister mine, you do not understand. You are too good and trustful. This fellow turns up from the Lord knows where, and is treated like a king. Naturally the tiger has no wish to become a mouse again.[1] And he has evidently discovered that there is nothing like a tear or two to soften your heart.'

Nilkanta hurriedly left the spot. He felt he would like to be a knife to cut Satish to pieces ; a needle to pierce him through and through ; a fire to burn him to ashes. But Satish was not even scarred. It was only his own heart that bled and bled.

Satish had brought with him from Calcutta a grand inkstand. The inkpot was set in a mother-of-pearl boat drawn by a German-silver goose supporting a penholder. It was a great favourite of his, and he cleaned it carefully every day with an old silk handkerchief. Kiran would laugh and, tapping the silver bird's beak, would say—

> Twice-born bird, ah ! wherefore stirred
> To wrong our royal lady ?

---

[1] A reference to a folk-story of a saint who turned a pet mouse into a tiger.

and the usual war of words would break out
between her and her brother-in-law.

The day before they were to start, the inkstand
was missing, and could nowhere be found.   Kiran
smiled, and said : ' Brother-in-law, your goose has
flown off to look for your Damaynti." [1]

But Satish was in a great rage.   He was certain
that Nilkanta had stolen it—for several people said
they had seen him prowling about the room the
night before.   He had the accused brought before
him.   Kiran also was there.   ' You have stolen
my inkstand, you thief ! ' he blurted out.   ' Bring
it back at once.'   Nilkanta had always taken
punishment from Sharat, deserved or undeserved,
with perfect equanimity.   But, when he was called
a thief in Kiran's presence, his eyes blazed with a
fierce anger, his breast swelled, and his throat
choked.   If Satish had said another word he would
have flown at him like a wild cat, and used his nails
like claws.

Kiran was greatly distressed at the scene, and
taking the boy into another room said in her sweet,
kind way : ' Nilu, if you really have taken that
inkstand give it to me quietly, and I shall see that
no one says another word to you about it.'   Big

[1] To find Satish a wife.

tears coursed down the boy's cheeks, till at last he hid his face in his hands, and wept bitterly. Kiran came back from the room, and said : 'I am sure Nilkanta has not taken the inkstand.' Sharat and Satish were equally positive that no other than Nilkanta could have done it.

But Kiran said determinedly : 'Never.'

Sharat wanted to cross-examine the boy, but his wife refused to allow it.

Then Satish suggested that his room and box should be searched. And Kiran said : 'If you dare do such a thing I will never, never forgive you. You shall not spy on the poor innocent boy.' And as she spoke, her wonderful eyes filled with tears. That settled the matter, and effectually prevented any further molestation of Nilkanta!

Kiran's heart overflowed with pity at this attempted outrage on a homeless lad. She got two new suits of clothes and a pair of shoes, and with these and a banknote in her hand she quietly went into Nilkanta's room in the evening. She intended to put these parting presents into his box as a surprise. The box itself had been her gift.

From her bunch of keys she selected one that fitted, and noiselessly opened the box. It was so jumbled up with odds and ends that the new clothes would not go in. So she thought she had better take everything out and pack the box for him. At first knives, tops, kite-flying reels, bamboo twigs, polished shells for peeling green mangoes, bottoms of broken tumblers and such like things dear to a boy's heart were discovered. Then there came a layer of linen, clean and other-wise. And from under the linen there emerged the missing inkstand, goose and all!

Kiran, with flushed face, sat down helplessly with the inkstand in her hand, puzzled and wondering.

In the meantime, Nilkanta had come into the room from behind without Kiran knowing it. He had seen the whole thing, and thought that Kiran had come like a thief to catch him in his thieving, — and that his deed was out. How could he ever hope to convince her that he was not a thief, and that only revenge had prompted him to take the inkstand, which he meant to throw into the river at the first chance? In a weak moment he had put it in his box instead. 'He was not a thief,' his heart cried out, 'not a thief!' Then what was he? What could he say? He had stolen, and yet he was not a thief! He could never explain to Kiran how grievously wrong

she was in taking him for a thief ; how could he
bear the thought that she had tried to spy on him?

At last Kiran with a deep sigh replaced the
inkstand in the box, and, as if she were the thief
herself, covered it up with the linen and the
trinkets as they were before ; and at the top she
placed the presents together with the banknote
which she had brought for him.

The next day the boy was nowhere to be found.
The villagers had not seen him ; the police could
discover no trace of him. Said Sharat : ' Now,
as a matter of curiosity, let us have a look at
his box.' But Kiran was obstinate in her refusal
to allow that to be done.

She had the box brought up to her own room ;
and taking out the inkstand alone, threw it into
the river.

The whole family went home. In a day the
garden became desolate. And only that starving
mongrel of Nilkanta's remained prowling along
the river-bank, whining and whining as if its heart
would break.

SAVED

SAVED

GOURI was the beautiful, delicately nurtured child
of an old and wealthy family. Her husband,
Paresh, had recently by his own efforts improved
his straitened circumstances. So long as he
was poor, Gouri's parents had kept their daughter
at home, unwilling to surrender her to privation ;
so she was no longer young when at last she went
to her husband's house. And Paresh never felt
quite that she belonged to him. He was an
advocate in a small western town, and had
no close kinsman with him. All his thought
was about his wife, so much so that sometimes
he would come home before the rising of the
Court. At first Gouri was at a loss to understand
why he came back suddenly. Sometimes, too, he
would dismiss one of the servants without reason ;
none of them ever suited him long. Especially
if Gouri desired to keep any particular servant
because he was useful, that man was sure to be

got rid of forthwith. The high-spirited Gouri greatly resented this, but her resentment only made her husband's behaviour still stranger.

At last when Paresh, unable to contain himself any longer, began in secret to cross-question the maid about her, the whole thing reached his wife's ears. She was a woman of few words; but her pride raged within like a wounded lioness at these insults, and this mad suspicion swept like a destroyer's sword between them. Paresh, as soon as he saw that his wife understood his motive, felt no more delicacy about taxing Gouri to her face; and the more his wife treated it with silent contempt, the more did the fire of his jealousy consume him.

Deprived of wedded happiness, the childless Gouri betook herself to the consolations of religion. She sent for Paramananda Swami, the young preacher of the Prayer-House hard by, and, formally acknowledging him as her spiritual preceptor, asked him to expound the *Gita* to her. All the wasted love and affection of her woman's heart was poured out in reverence at the feet of her Guru.

No one had any doubts about the purity of Paramananda's character. All worshipped him. And because Paresh did not dare to hint at any suspicion against him, his jealousy ate its way into his heart like a hidden cancer.

One day some trifling circumstance made the poison overflow. Paresh reviled Paramananda to his wife as a hypocrite, and said: 'Can you swear that you are not in love with this crane that plays the ascetic?'

Gouri sprang up like a snake that has been trodden on, and, maddened by his suspicion, said with bitter irony: 'And what if I am?' At this Paresh forthwith went off to the Court-house, and locked the door on her.

In a white heat of passion at this last outrage, Gouri got the door open somehow, and left the house.

Paramananda was poring over the scriptures in his lonely room in the silence of noon. All at once, like a flash of lightning out of a cloudless sky, Gouri broke in upon his reading.

'You here?' questioned her Guru in surprise.

'Rescue me, O my lord Guru,' said she, 'from the insults of my home life, and allow me to dedicate myself to the service of your feet.'

With a stern rebuke, Paramananda sent Gouri back home. But I wonder whether he ever again took up the snapped thread of his reading.

Paresh, finding the door open, on his return home, asked: 'Who has been here?'

P

'No one!' his wife replied. '*I* have been to the house of my Guru.'

'Why?' asked Paresh, pale and red by turns.

'Because I wanted to.'

From that day Paresh had a guard kept over the house, and behaved so absurdly that the tale of his jealousy was told all over the town.

The news of the shameful insults that were daily heaped on his disciple disturbed the religious meditations of Paramananda. He felt he ought to leave the place at once; at the same time he could not make up his mind to forsake the tortured woman. Who can say how the poor ascetic got through those terrible days and nights?

At last one day the imprisoned Gouri got a letter. 'My child,' it ran, 'it is true that many holy women have left the world to devote themselves to God. Should it happen that the trials of this world are driving your thoughts away from God, I will with God's help rescue his handmaid for the holy service of his feet. If you desire, you may meet me by the tank in your garden at two o'clock to-morrow afternoon.'

Gouri hid the letter in the loops of her hair. At noon next day when she was undoing her hair before her bath she found that the letter was not there. Could it have fallen on to the bed and got into her husband's hands, she wondered. At first, she felt a kind of fierce pleasure in thinking that it would enrage him ; and then she could not bear to think that this letter, worn as a halo of deliverance on her head, might be defiled by the touch of insolent hands.

With swift steps she hurried to her husband's room. He lay groaning on the floor, with eyes rolled back and foaming mouth. She detached the letter from his clenched fist, and sent quickly for a doctor.

The doctor said it was a case of apoplexy. The patient had died before his arrival.

That very day, as it happened, Paresh had an important appointment away from home. Paramananda had found this out, and accordingly had made his appointment with Gouri. To such a depth had he fallen !

When the widowed Gouri caught sight from the window of her Guru stealing like a thief to the side of the pool, she lowered her eyes as at a lightning flash. And in that flash she saw clearly what a fall his had been.

The Guru called : ' Gouri.'

' I am coming,' she replied.

．　　　．　　　．　　　．　　　．　　　．

When Paresh's friends heard of his death, and came to assist in the last rites, they found the dead body of Gouri lying beside that of her husband. She had poisoned herself. All were lost in admiration of the wifely loyalty she had shown in her *sati*, a loyalty rare indeed in these degenerate days.

MY FAIR NEIGHBOUR

MY FAIR NEIGHBOUR

My feelings towards the young widow who lived in the next house to mine were feelings of worship ; at least, that is what I told to my friends and myself. Even my nearest intimate, Nabin, knew nothing of the real state of my mind. And I had a sort of pride that I could keep my passion pure by thus concealing it in the inmost recesses of my heart. She was like a dew-drenched *sephali*-blossom, untimely fallen to earth. Too radiant and holy for the flower-decked marriage-bed, she had been dedicated to Heaven.

But passion is like the mountain stream, and refuses to be enclosed in the place of its birth ; it must seek an outlet. That is why I tried to give expression to my emotions in poems ; but my unwilling pen refused to desecrate the object of my worship.

It happened curiously that just at this time my friend Nabin was afflicted with a madness of verse.   It came upon him like an earthquake.   It was the poor fellow's first attack, and he was equally unprepared for rhyme and rhythm.   Nevertheless he could not refrain, for he succumbed to the fascination, as a widower to his second wife.

So Nabin sought help from me.   The subject of his poems was the old, old one, which is ever new : his poems were all addressed to the beloved one. I slapped his back in jest, and asked him : ' Well, old chap, who is she ? '

Nabin laughed, as he replied : ' That I have not yet discovered ! '

I confess that I found considerable comfort in bringing help to my friend.   Like a hen brooding on a duck's egg, I lavished all the warmth of my pent-up passion on Nabin's effusions.   So vigorously did I revise and improve his crude productions, that the larger part of each poem became my own.

Then Nabin would say in surprise : ' That is just what I wanted to say, but could not.   How on earth do you manage to get hold of all these fine sentiments ? '

Poet-like, I would reply : ' They come from my imagination ; for, as you know, truth is silent, and it is imagination only which waxes eloquent. Reality represses the flow of feeling like a rock ; imagination cuts out a path for itself.'

And the poor puzzled Nabin would say : ' Y-e-s, I see, yes, of course ' ; and then after some thought would murmur again : ' Yes, yes, you are right ! '

As I have already said, in my own love there was a feeling of reverential delicacy which prevented me from putting it into words.   But with Nabin as a screen, there was nothing to hinder the flow of my pen ; and a true warmth of feeling gushed out into these vicarious poems.

Nabin in his lucid moments would say : ' But these are yours ! Let me publish them over your name.'

' Nonsense ! ' I would reply.   ' They are yours, my dear fellow ; I have only added a touch or two here and there.'

And Nabin gradually came to believe it.

I will not deny that, with a feeling akin to that of the astronomer gazing into the starry heavens, I did sometimes turn my eyes towards the window of the house next door.   It is also true that now and again my furtive glances would be rewarded with a vision.   And the least glimpse of the pure light of that countenance would at once still and clarify all that was turbulent and unworthy in my emotions.

But one day I was startled. Could I believe my eyes ? It was a hot summer afternoon. One of the fierce and fitful nor'-westers was threatening. Black clouds were massed in the north-west corner of the sky ; and against the strange and fearful light of that background my fair neighbour stood, gazing out into empty space. And what a world of forlorn longing did I discover in the far-away look of those lustrous black eyes ! Was there then, perchance, still some living volcano within the serene radiance of that moon of mine ? Alas ! that look of limitless yearning, which was winging its way through the clouds like an eager bird, surely sought—not heaven—but the nest of some human heart !

At the sight of the unutterable passion of that look I could hardly contain myself. I was no longer satisfied with correcting crude poems. My whole being longed to express itself in some worthy action. At last I thought I would devote myself to making widow - remarriage popular in my country. I was prepared not only to speak and write on the subject, but also to spend money on its cause.

Nabin began to argue with me. 'Permanent widowhood,' said he, 'has in it a sense of immense purity and peace; a calm beauty like that of the silent places of the dead shimmering in the wan light of the eleventh moon.[1] Would not the mere possibility of remarriage destroy its divine beauty?'

Now this sort of sentimentality always makes me furious. In time of famine, if a well-fed man speaks scornfully of food, and advises a starving man at point of death to glut his hunger on the fragrance of flowers and the song of birds, what are we to think of him? I said with some heat: 'Look here, Nabin, to the artist a ruin may be a beautiful object; but houses are built not only for the contemplation of artists, but that people may live therein; so they have to be kept in repair in spite of artistic susceptibilities. It is all very well for you to idealise widowhood from your safe distance, but you should remember that within widowhood there is a sensitive human heart, throbbing with pain and desire.'

I had an impression that the conversion of Nabin would be a difficult matter, so perhaps I

[1] The eleventh day of the moon is a day of fasting and penance.

was more impassioned than I need have been.   I
was somewhat surprised to find at the conclusion
of my little speech that Nabin after a single
thoughtful sigh completely agreed with me.   The
even more convincing peroration which I felt I
might have delivered was not needed !

After about a week Nabin came to me, and
said that if I would help him he was prepared to
lead the way by marrying a widow himself.

I was overjoyed.   I embraced him effusively,
and promised him any money that might be required for the purpose.   Then Nabin told me his
story.

I learned that Nabin's loved one was not an
imaginary being.   It appeared that Nabin, too,
had for some time adored a widow from a distance,
but had not spoken of his feelings to any living
soul.   Then the magazines in which Nabin's
poems, or rather *my* poems, used to appear had
reached the fair one's hands ; and the poems had
not been ineffective.

Not that Nabin had deliberately intended, as
he was careful to explain, to conduct love-making
in that way.   In fact, said he, he had no idea
that the widow knew how to read.   He used to
post the magazine, without disclosing the sender's

name, addressed to the widow's brother. It was only a sort of fancy of his, a concession to his hopeless passion. It was flinging garlands before a deity ; it is not the worshipper's affair whether the god knows or not, whether he accepts or ignores the offering.

And Nabin particularly wanted me to understand that he had no definite end in view when on diverse pretexts he sought and made the acquaintance of the widow's brother. Any near relation of the loved one needs must have a special interest for the lover.

Then followed a long story about how an illness of the brother at last brought them together. The presence of the poet himself naturally led to much discussion of the poems ; nor was the discussion necessarily restricted to the subject out of which it arose.

After his recent defeat in argument at my hands, Nabin had mustered up courage to propose marriage to the widow. At first he could not gain her consent. But when he had made full use of my eloquent words, supplemented by a tear or two of his own, the fair one capitulated unconditionally. Some money was now wanted by her guardian to make arrangements.

'Take it at once,' said I.

'But,' Nabin went on, 'you know it will be some months before I can appease my father sufficiently for him to continue my allowance. How are we to live in the meantime?' I wrote out the necessary cheque without a word, and then I said: 'Now tell me who she is. You need not look on me as a possible rival, for I swear I will not write poems to her; and even if I do I will not send them to her brother, but to you!'

'Don't be absurd,' said Nabin; 'I have not kept back her name because I feared your rivalry! The fact is, she was very much perturbed at taking this unusual step, and had asked me not to talk about the matter to my friends. But it no longer matters, now that everything has been satisfactorily settled. She lives at No. 19, the house next to yours.'

If my heart had been an iron boiler it would have burst. 'So she has no objection to re-marriage?' I simply asked.

'Not at the present moment,' replied Nabin with a smile.

'And was it the poems alone which wrought the magic change?'

'Well, my poems were not so bad, you know,' said Nabin, 'were they?'

I swore mentally.

But at whom was I to swear?   At him?   At myself?   At Providence?   All the same, I swore.

THE END